A KISS FOR LORD CHALLMOND

"Have you no sense?" he demanded in exasperation. "A young lady does not gad about the countryside without a groom or at least her maid."

"I have been gadding about, as you put it, since I was able to walk."

"You are no longer a scrapegrace child," he pointed out. "There are dangers for a young maiden that only a fool would ignore."

"I do not need lectures on my behavior from a known rake, Lord Challmond."

"Why, you hellion," Simon breathed, caught between the desire to shake some sense into her and kiss her. Stepping forward he grasped her upper arms. "I should teach you a lesson in placing yourself at the mercy of scoundrels."

Claire's magnificent eyes darkened, but her courage never failed. "Unhand me."

Knowing he was behaving badly, Simon was nevertheless unable to resist the temptation to taste the delicate softness of her lips. . . .

Books by Debbie Raleigh

LORD CARLTON'S COURTSHIP

LORD MUMFORD'S MINX

A BRIDE FOR LORD CHALLMOND

Published by Zebra Books

A BRIDE
FOR LORD
CHALLMOND

Debbie Raleigh

ZEBRA BOOKS
Kensington Publishing Corp.

http://www.zebrabooks.com

ZEBRA BOOKS are published by

Kensington Publishing Corp.
850 Third Avenue
New York, NY 10022

All Kensington titles, imprints and distributed lines are available at special quantity discounts for bulk purchases for sales promotions, premiums, fund raising, educational or institutional use.

Special book excerpts or customized printings can also be created to fit specific needs. For details, write or phone the office of the Kensington Special Sales Manager: Kensington Publishing Corp., 850 Third Avenue, New York, NY, 10022. Attn. Special Sales Department. Phone: 1-800-221-2647.

Zebra and the Z logo Reg. U.S. Pat. & TM Off.

First Printing: January, 2001
10 9 8 7 6 5 4 3 2 1

Printed in the United States of America

TO THE HEROS IN MY LIFE
DAVID, CHANCE, ALEXANDER AND DON

AND TO
MOM AND DAD
WHO ALWAYS BELIEVED

Prologue

The three dashing gentlemen attracted more than their share of attention as they rode through the Italian countryside. Tall, handsome, and in possession of that rare arrogance that comes from wealth and position, they were the darlings of the small British society that had recently flocked to Rome.

It was a position they relished after the brutal hardship of war. Forming a select guard that had escorted the Pope in his return to the Vatican, they had lingered into the summer months, enjoying the splendid entertainments and luscious local ladies. And in truth, none of the three was in any hurry to return to England despite the fact they had sold out their commissions.

Time enough to return to the responsibilities that awaited them at home. For now they wished only to rejoice in the pleasure of being alive.

Simon Townsled, seventh Earl of Challmond, sucked in a deep breath of the scented air.

Overhead, the impossibly blue sky shimmered with the summer heat. It was a heat he welcomed. Since being wounded several weeks before, he often battled a persistent chill.

Now he lifted his dark, aquiline countenance to the sunshine. In the distance he could hear the echo of angry shouts, but it was not until a sharp scream pierced the air that he was shaken from his pleasant daydreams.

Pulling the large mount to a halt, he turned to regard his companions with a startled expression.

"What the devil?"

"Damn," Barth Juston, Lord Wickton, cursed as he pointed toward the nearby field.

Simon shifted in his saddle to view the half dozen roughly dressed men that appeared to be circling a—by gads, it appeared to be an old woman.

Realization hit the same moment another scream echoed through the air.

A fierce scowl marred the elegant beauty of Philip Marrow, Lord Brasleigh's, features.

"Come," he commanded as he urged his stallion into a full gallop.

Simon and Barth were not far behind. Together they plunged through the overgrown field toward the small crowd. At a signal from Philip the three split apart, rounding the unaware men and approaching from different angles. It was a tactic they had used in battle, and not surprisingly they easily managed to charge through the crowd and place themselves between the men and the elderly woman now huddled beside a large rock.

Simon withdrew a pistol and shot it into the air, hoping to frighten the men off. Although he was an excellent marksman, he dearly hoped he would have no need to defend himself. He had seen enough blood for a lifetime.

"Move along," he commanded in stern tones. "Find your sport elsewhere."

For a moment the men glared at the intruders, clearly debating whether to challenge the mounted gentlemen. Then, noting the hard expressions and military bearing, they reluctantly began backing away.

Simon held his breath as more than one raised a fist to shake it in his direction, but realizing their sport was at an end, they retreated toward a nearby village.

Barth was already off his horse and helping the shaken woman to her feet. Simon and Philip dismounted to join him, exchanging a silent glance as they recognized the tattered clothing of a Gypsy.

That certainly explained the reason for the attack, Simon thought with a sigh. Locals often blamed their troubles on the Gypsies. Old customs and superstitions died hard.

"Are you hurt?" Barth demanded, his rakish countenance uncommonly somber as he gently helped the old woman to her feet.

"No." The woman offered them a tentative

smile as she brushed the twigs and dirt from her skirt. *"Grazie."*

Still on alert, Philip glanced toward the cluster of buildings atop the nearby hill.

"We should get her away from the village."

Barth gave a sharp nod of his head. "Can you lead us to your home?"

The woman's smile widened. *"Sí.* I lead."

She turned and began making her way toward the thicket of woods, and after a pause the three men collected their horses and followed behind. None of them needed Philip's signal to keep their guards up as they entered the fringe of trees. Only a fool would not suspect that this all had been a clever trap.

Moving through the dappled shadows, the three kept the woman in sight as she easily slipped through the trees. Bringing up the rear, Simon ensured there were no unpleasant surprises from behind. So intent on his watch, it came as a distinct surprise when they rounded a corner and abruptly landed in the midst of a large camp.

The three gentlemen held their pistols ready as a dozen men and women poured from the covered wagon to gather about the elderly woman. For a tense moment Simon held himself at alert, but as their chatter filled the air, he at last accepted they had all but been forgotten by the Gypsies. With a signal from Philip, Simon and his companions backed toward the edge of the small glade.

"I believe this is home," Barth murmured. Simon nodded. "Shall we go?"

"There is little use in remaining," Philip decided. "It is getting late and I have a particularly enticing widow awaiting my attention in Rome."

"Not as enticing as my barmaid, I'll wager," Barth teased.

"Wait. Please." Without warning, a young, decidedly lovely woman with dark hair and flashing eyes appeared before them. "Grandmother wishes to thank you."

"There is no need," Philip retorted.

"Please." She smiled, her hands waving toward a fallen tree. "Have a seat."

The three glanced at one another before giving a rueful shrug and settling themselves on the log. Simon was as eager as his friends to return to Rome and the delights of a willing upstairs maid, but he had no wish to offend the old woman, who had already suffered enough for one afternoon. With a sigh he impatiently awaited the dead lizard that was supposedly a lucky charm or the Gypsy cards that would foretell their future. Within moments the old woman returned, but surprisingly she carried a perfect red rose clutched in her gnarled hands.

Simon lifted his brows as she approached each one of them, brushing the velvet bloom over their foreheads and muttering words in a strange language. At last done, she stepped back and offered them a wide smile.

Philip frowned toward the young woman standing to one side.

"What is this?"

"A blessing."

"What did she say?" Barth demanded.

"She says:

> *A love that is true*
> *A heart that is steady*
> *A wounded soul healed*
> *A spirit made ready.*
> *Three women will come*
> *As the seasons will turn*
> *And bring true love to each*
> *Before the summer again burns* .

You are very fortunate. Grandmother has blessed you with the gift of true love."

An explosive silence followed the softly spoken words. Then, almost as one, the three gentlemen burst into disbelieving laughter.

Although it was only mid-February, the discreet London gambling establishment was filled with elegant gentlemen. Seated in a distant corner, Philip, Barth, and Simon shared their second decanter of brandy. By the end of the month Simon would be in Devonshire and Barth would be in Kent. They intended to enjoy the brief time they had left together.

Simon filled his glass and lifted it in mocking salute.

"What shall we drink to?"

"Lovely ladies," Barth retorted, no doubt thinking of the opera dancer awaiting him across town.

"The more the merrier," Philip added.

"So much for the Gypsy's blessing." Simon took a large drink of the amber liquid.

"Blessing?" Barth snorted. "Curse more like it."

"Ah, but the heat of summer has not yet come," Philip drawled.

Barth gave a startled blink. Of the three of them, Philip was by far the most cynical.

"You do not believe in such nonsense?"

"True love?" Philip's handsome features twisted. "Fah."

"I do not know. I loved Fiona this afternoon." Simon gave a low chuckle as he recalled his beautiful mistress and her reaction to his confession he was leaving for Devonshire. She possessed little sympathy for his odd ache to return to his vast estate. "Until she threw that vase at my head."

Barth refilled his glass. "Casanova had the right of it. Love is meant to be shared with as many willing beauties as possible."

Philip abruptly rose to his feet. "Let us make a wager."

"A wager?" Simon demanded.

"Let us say . . . a thousand pounds and a

red rose to be paid the first day of June to the fool who succumbs to the Gypsy's curse."

"A thousand pounds?" Barth growled.

Philip eyed him with a twisted smile. "Not frightened that you might succumb to the wiles of a mere female, are you, Barth?"

"You forget, I am about to be wed. How can a gentleman find true love when he is shackled to necessity?"

"Simon?"

Simon shrugged. Even if he believed in the fable of true love, he was hardly likely to discover it in the wilds of Devonshire.

"I have no fear."

"Then we shall meet here the first day of June." Philip waited for Simon and Barth to rise to their feet and touch their glass to his own. "To the Casanova Club. Long may it prosper."

One

Cresting the edge of the hill, the two gentlemen pulled their mounts to a halt. Below them the stately manor house consumed an awe-inspiring amount of the pristine parkland with stark lines and sweeping wings. Only the balustrades with fluted columns and Ionic portico provided relief from the classic simplicity. It was an overwhelming view. Even Simon Townsled, seventh Earl of Challmond, who had resided at the Devonshire estate since he was a lad of twelve, found his breath catching in his throat.

How long had it been since he had lived at Westwood Park? Oh, not the dutiful appearances to visit his elderly cousin or, since the sixth earl's death, the flamboyant hunting parties he had hosted. But to actually reside at the estate? It had been years.

But oddly, during the heat of battle it had been this place he had longed to see.

The magnificent black stallion shifted with a restless dissatisfaction at having his gallop in-

terrupted, and Simon allowed a sudden smile
to slash across his thin countenance. Although
not a precisely handsome gentleman, there
was a decided charm to his tousled auburn
locks and emerald eyes sprinkled with gold.
And more than one lover had claimed there
was the devil's own charm in his flashing dim-
ples. He was uncertain what odd compulsion
had urged him to Devonshire, but he had arrived and he intended to make the best of his
visit.

"There you are, Locky." He shifted to regard the short, bluntly built gentleman at his
side. Unlike Simon's own elegant breeches and
fitted coat, Mr. James Lockmeade's outfit con-
sisted of plain buckskins with boots that had
seen better days. It would be hard to determine from his appearance that his grandfather
was one of the wealthiest merchants in all of
England, or that his mother was the daughter
of an earl. He was a plain-spoken man with
few airs and a decided lack of pretensions. Simon had met Locky when he had joined his
regiment. While others had dismissed the
large man's abrupt speech and methodical
manner as a sign of his unsavory connections
to the shop, Simon had been immediately impressed with the young man's unwavering
courage. When far more nobly born men had
fled in panic, Locky had stood as firm as a
mountain, and it had been only his staunch
nerve that had saved Simon when he had

been wounded during a skirmish with the Frenchies. Nearly unconscious, Simon had been unable to stand or defend himself as his commander had called for a retreat. It had been Locky who had slung him over his shoulder as Lord Wickton and Lord Brasleigh had carved a path through the battle lines to freedom. Without the three of them Simon would have been just another peer sacrificed for duty and Crown. "Westwood Park, county seat to the earls of Challmond for the past one hundred years."

The square, ruddy-tinted countenance grimaced. "Good God," he at last pronounced.

Simon gave a pleased chuckle. There were few not overwhelmed by the grandeur of Westwood Park.

"Yes, indeed."

"The devil take it, Simon," Locky growled, "I shall feel a fool rattling about like a bloody nob."

Simon shrugged. Although Locky had never spoken much of his past, he had suspected the young man was much like himself. A puppet torn between two worlds and never quite fitting into either one.

"You shall soon become accustomed."

"Aye." Locky appeared far from convinced.

Simon gave another laugh. "In any event, we shall devote ourselves to thinning the local trout population."

"See that we do," Locky muttered darkly.

"Come." Loosening his grip on his reins, Simon allowed his mount to continue his gallop through the meadow to the waiting stable below. Handing the reins to a wide-eyed lad, he led the way to the main house. Despite the fact he had given no warning of his impending arrival the door was pulled open by his impeccably attired butler. Simon had never doubted for a moment the estate would be in pristine condition. The previous earl had demanded total devotion from his large staff and would tolerate nothing less than perfection. "Ah, Calvert."

The tall, gaunt-faced servant with silver hair performed a crisp bow.

"My lord, welcome home."

Stepping into the black and white marble foyer, Simon glanced up at the large coat of arms that hung above the arched door to the main hall. Just for a moment he recalled being a terrified young lad as he had stood in this hall, waiting to meet the man who would teach him to become the next Earl of Challmond. It was a memory he swiftly dismissed as he turned back to the butler. The days of bleak loneliness and uncertainty were in the past. He was a gentleman with his destiny firmly in his grasp.

"Thank you, Calvert, it is good to be back." He waved his hand toward his silent companion. "And this is Mr. Lockmeade. The gentleman who saved my life."

Locky immediately flushed with embarrassment. "Bah."

"Show Mr. Lockmeade to the blue room and have a bath drawn."

Without displaying a hint of displeasure that his master had arrived without so much as a note of warning and brought along a guest, Calvert gave a nod of his head.

"Very good, my lord."

Simon flashed his friend an encouraging smile. "I put you in capable hands, Locky. I shall meet you for a brandy in the library before we dine."

Locky grimaced. "If I can find the bloody library."

"I shall have Calvert sketch you a map."

"Have him send a carriage," Locky countered with a gleam in his dark eyes. "I shall no doubt have to track halfway back to London to find my bedchamber."

Simon chuckled. "Chin up, old chap."

With a half-mocking bow Locky turned and allowed the butler to lead him up the large curving staircase. On his own, Simon tossed his hat and gloves onto an ebony table inlaid with ivory and made his way through the main hall. He could use a bath and rest himself after his long ride, but his feet determinedly carried him to the last doorway and into the sprawling library.

A tiny pang tugged at his heart as he stepped in and glanced at the book-lined walls

and heavy black chimney piece flanked by
matching wing chairs. The scent of aged
leather forcibly reminded him of the old earl
and the days he had spent carefully tutoring
the young Simon in the intricate details of
managing the vast estate. He had been a stern
taskmaster who had offered little compassion
for Simon's tender age or his wrenching desire
to return to his own large, boisterous family,
but in retrospect Simon forced himself to ac-
knowledge that the old earl had simply done
what he thought best for his heir.

Now he moved across the Persian carpet to
peer through the open French doors at the
garden. Although it was early March, the beds
were well tended with a few spring blooms,
adding a touch of color to the formal hedges
and sparkling fountains. A faint sound behind
him had Simon spinning about to watch the
thin, gray-haired housekeeper step into the
room.

"My lord, welcome home." She regarded
him with obvious pleasure.

Home?

Was he home?

For that matter, what was home?

This vast estate? His elegant town house in
London? The derelict, overcrowded vicarage of
his parents?

Perhaps none of them was truly his home.

What had Philip said?

"A gentleman should never become overly

attached to a woman or a home. They were both demanding masters that would steal a man's soul. . . ."

With a mental shrug Simon forced a smile to his lips. The older woman was clearly pleased at his arrival, and the least he could do was pretend he was just as delighted to be there.

"Thank you, Mrs. King."

"Can I bring you tea?"

"That would be lovely."

"Cook is making your favorite scones." The older woman narrowed her gaze as she studied Simon's slender form. "A good thing too. You appear half starved."

Simon took no offense at the servant's familiar manner. Mrs. King had been the closest he had to a mother when he had come to Westwood Park.

"I was certainly not so well fed as I am here," he admitted.

"I should think not," Mrs. King sniffed. "What does the army know of caring for a proper gentleman?"

Simon grimaced at the harsh memories of the past two years.

"Precious little, I assure you. Thankfully that is all in the past."

A hint of contentment settled about the housekeeper. "And Calvert tells me that we have a guest."

"Yes, indeed, a Mr. Lockmeade."

"How long shall the gentleman be staying?"

"For as long as I can convince him to remain. Which, unfortunately, will probably not be for long."

"Will there be any other guests joining us?"

"Good God, I hope not," Simon retorted. His brief stay in London after returning from Italy had been quite enough socializing for Simon. Odd for a gentleman who had once spent the majority of the year in London.

"I see." Mrs. King allowed only a small flicker of disappointment to show before giving a decisive nod of her head. "I will see to your tea."

"Thank you, Mrs. King."

Simon watched as the older woman left the room, then turned back toward the open French doors. The inviting afternoon sunshine lured him onto the paved terrace, and within moments he wandered toward the shallow steps. It was the distant sound of raised voices that had him turning toward the far side of the garden, and he gave a sudden exclamation at the sight of the two figures just beyond the hedge.

"What the devil?"

More curious than alarmed, Simon marched along the narrow path toward the intruders. Within moments he had recognized the large, grisly steward he had hired before buying his commission, but it was the slender maiden with glossy raven curls and entrancing blue eyes that captured his attention.

She was exquisite, he acknowledged. Such delicately carved features and skin of the purest silk. Even with her hands planted on her hips and a frown marring her brow she made his blood quicken. A dark-haired angel that he fully intended to become better acquainted with.

Coming to a halt, Simon regarded the two with raised brows.

"Foster, would you care to explain what is occurring?"

Two heads turned to regard him with varying degrees of surprise. Foster was the first to recover as his thick features reddened while the unknown maiden merely allowed her glare to shift to him.

"Oh . . . my lord." The steward gave a hasty bow. "Welcome home."

"Is something the matter?"

"Nothing of importance, my lord."

"Nothing of importance?" The woman gave a sharp noise of disapproval. "You consider allowing cottages to fall into ruin as nothing of importance?"

Simon blinked, uncertain of what he had expected. He had sensed the two had been arguing but certainly not about cottages.

"What?"

The steward gave a nervous laugh. "The lady exaggerates, my lord."

"Ha. I have just come from the Andersons',
where a portion of their wall gave way and
nearly injured their baby," the lady accused.

Foster's flush deepened. "Absurd."

"I suppose you also claim that it is absurd
that Mrs. Foley is more in hope of remaining
dry by standing beneath a tree than in her
own home?"

"This ain't be none of your concern," Foster
growled, clearly furious with the audacious
chit.

Decidedly confused by the odd encounter,
Simon turned toward the strange maiden.
Beautiful she might be, but she had no right
to trespass upon his land and accuse his steward of neglecting his duties.

"Frankly, I must agree with my steward,
miss . . . ?"

Undaunted, the woman narrowed her glittering gaze.

"Unfortunately I am not surprised."

Simon's brows arched even higher. "Pardon
me?"

"Clearly you are indifferent to your estate if
you are willing to leave it in the hands of this
pitiful, wholly incompetent fool."

"Now, see here . . ." Foster sputtered.

Simon's own gaze narrowed. Although not
overly puffed up with his own importance, Simon was nevertheless accustomed to a degree
of respect for his position and wealth. He was
rather annoyed by the woman's sharp insult.

"Foster, perhaps you should go about your duties."

"But, my lord . . ."

"We will discuss this later," he assured the disgruntled steward.

There was no mistaking the authority in Simon's tone, and with a covert glare at the slender intruder the servant gave a reluctant nod of his head.

"Very well."

Simon waited until Foster had stomped toward the distant greenhouse before turning to stab the woman with a piercing gaze.

"Now, miss. Perhaps you would not mind explaining your presence on my estate?"

Blue eyes, as blue as an Italian sky, met his gaze squarely.

"I am here out of concern for your tenants," she announced in firm tones. "A concern, Lord Challmond, you clearly do not share."

Simon's annoyance deepened at the chit's accusations. What the devil did she know of his concern or lack of concern?

"I fail to comprehend how you could have the least notion of whether I am concerned or not for my tenants, considering that I have returned to Westwood Park less than an hour ago."

Expecting the lady to wilt beneath his chiding tone, he was caught off guard when her hands returned to her hips in a defiant motion.

"That is precisely the point. If you cared, you would reside here and tend to their needs."

Why, the bold little jade, he thought with a flare of exasperated humor.

"In case you are thoroughly witless, please allow me to inform you that a devious little Corsican by the name of Napoleon has been ravaging the Continent."

A delightful hint of color bloomed beneath her pale skin at his mocking words.

"I am well aware of Napoleon, my lord," she gritted out. "I am also aware that you left Oxford and headed straight for London, where you remained until buying your commission. In the meantime, Mr. Foster has managed to thoroughly abuse his position and what few loyal tenants you still possess live in conditions unfit for your livestock."

A sudden absurd flare of guilt rushed through Simon. It was true he had handed complete control of his estate to Mr. Foster. And that his attentions had been more devoted to the pleasures of London than to the condition of his cottages. But he certainly had no intention of being lectured for his behavior by this pint-sized termagant.

With a deliberate manner he lowered his gaze to the mud clinging to the hem of her pale lemon gown.

"Do you happen to be one of my tenants?" he politely inquired.

She caught her breath at his insult but refused to back down.

"Thankfully, no."

"Then, why are you so interested in their welfare?"

"They are human beings with the right to expect a decent home and food on their table."

"Certainly. Which is precisely what I ordered Foster to provide," he retorted. Did she think that he would intentionally wish to see his tenants neglected?

The blue eyes flashed. "Well, he failed miserably."

"If that is the case, then I shall soon have it set to right." He made a silent promise to make a thorough inspection of the estate the next morning. He was beginning to suspect that there was more to this woman's ranting than simply being a bit daft. "But you still have not answered my question."

"Question?"

"Who are you?"

There was a momentary pause before she heaved a reluctant sigh.

"Miss Blakewell."

"Blakewell?" Simon widened his eyes in surprise. This was Miss Blakewell? This was the grubby young girl who had once punched the squire's son when he had laughed at Simon's tears? The girl with tangled curls and a dirt-smudged countenance? Who the devil would have suspected such beauty hid beneath the dust? "Good God . . . Claire the Cat."

The now-lovely features hardened at the childish nickname. It had been given to her by the neighborhood boys who had been intimidated by her ready temper and habit of leaping to the defense of the vulnerable, whether it be a wounded bird or homesick young lad. It was an insult rarely said to her face, since she had bloodied more than one nose for lesser offenses.

Now her lips tightened, but she managed to resist the impulse to plant him a facer.

"I would prefer, my lord, if you did not refer to me by that hateful name."

Simon gave a sudden smile at her attempt to maintain a dignified composure. Well, well. Claire Blakewell. This was certainly a pleasant surprise.

"You have . . . changed," he murmured, his gaze lingering on the decided curve beneath the dark yellow pelisse.

"I should think so," she retorted in tart tones. "It has been, after all, nearly ten years since we last spoke."

He gave a low chuckle, his emerald eyes dancing.

"Of course, some things never change. Your tongue remains as sharp as ever."

She seemed to catch her breath at his boyish grin, then surprisingly her expression hardened with disapproval.

"And you are just as reluctant to shoulder the duties of Lord Challmond as you were at twelve."

Simon's smile abruptly faded. Damn, the woman was far too ready to strike where he was most vulnerable.

"Neither my duties nor my tenants are any of your concern."

"Then, you will do nothing to ease their suffering?"

"What I will do is return to the house for a warm bath and dinner with my guest. Tomorrow I will ride out and speak with my tenants." Simon was at his most arrogant. "I have little doubt I shall find them quite content."

Claire displayed all the stubborn tenacity she had possessed as a child.

"You shall find them ill used and quite terrified of Mr. Foster."

Unable to deny her accusations without further proof, Simon was forced to content himself with a negligent shrug.

"Time will tell. Now, if you will excuse me, I believe that Cook has prepared my favorite scones. She at least is pleased to have me back in Devonshire."

Miss Blakewell smiled without humor. " 'There are stranger things in heaven and earth . . .' " she quoted, then gave a toss of her head. "Good day, my lord."

Uncertain whether to laugh or be infuriated by the unexpected encounter, Simon was on

the point of turning back to the house, when
he realized that Miss Blakewell was inexplica-
bly alone.

"Did you come here on your own?"

"Certainly."

"Have you no sense?" he demanded in exasperation. He had been right in his first impression, he told himself. She was daft. "A
young lady does not gad about the countryside
without a groom or at least her maid."

Her chin tilted to a defiant angle. "I have
been gadding about, as you put it, since I was
able to walk."

That was true enough. Mr. Blakewell had always given his headstrong daughter far too
much freedom.

"You are no longer a scrapegrace child," he
pointed out in stern tones. "There are dangers
for a young maiden that only a fool would ignore."

She at least possessed the grace to blush. "I
do not need lectures on my behavior from a
known rake, Lord Challmond."

"Why, you hellion," Simon breathed, caught
between the desire to shake some sense into
her and kiss her. Stepping forward, he grasped
her upper arms. "I should teach you a lesson
in placing yourself at the mercy of scoundrels."

The magnificent eyes darkened, but her
courage never failed.

"Unhand me."

Knowing he was behaving badly, Simon was nevertheless unable to resist the temptation to taste the delicate softness of her lips. He felt her shiver and pulled her closer, his heart racing at the sweet innocence of her mouth. She was sunshine and honey, with a scent of lilac that was stirring a heat in his thighs. His lips pressed even deeper as he forgot he was merely teaching her a lesson in the dangers of men. It was not until he heard Claire give a low moan that he returned to his senses. With a silent curse he pulled back and gazed down at her flushed features.

"Lord Challmond . . . how dare you?" she at last managed to croak.

Simon wasn't certain how he dared, but he did know he was not remotely sorry for his shameful behavior. Indeed, he very much wished he possessed the nerve to do it again.

"It was a simple kiss, Miss Blakewell." He smiled with wry amusement. "Now perhaps you will consider the consequences of your willful behavior."

Unlike the dozens of young maidens Simon had encountered who would have fainted at his audacity, or coyly invited further attentions, Claire seared him with a blazing glare.

"Tend to your tenants, Lord Challmond. They are in need of your attentions. I most certainly am not."

Turning on her heel, Claire marched past

the hedge and disappeared. Standing in the garden, Simon gave a slow shake of his head.

Damnation, she was a most lovely creature.

Unbidden, the memory of the Gypsy brushing his forehead with a rose flashed through his mind.

True love awaited him. . . .

Fah.

The only thing that awaited him was a warm bath and his favorite scones.

TWO

Claire was in a fine temper.

Storming across the wide meadow that marched Westwood Park with the Blakewell estate, she brooded on Lord Challmond's audacious behavior.

How dare he?

She was no common tart in search of a protector. Or, worse, a London sophisticate wishing for a dalliance with the notorious rake. She was a respectable maiden with no interest in stolen kisses.

With a sharp motion she raised her hand to scrub her lips that still tingled from his touch. She did not want to consider the renegade flare of pleasure that had trembled through her body or the manner her heart had raced with excitement. She had been caught off guard. It was nothing more than shock that had caused her strange reactions.

Still, the sensible explanation did nothing to erase the lingering heat of his mouth or the memory of his boyishly charming features. How he had changed, she thought with an odd shiver. She could still recall the sad-eyed lad with too-large ears and a habit of hiding in the stables. She could also recall the hint of wounded vulnerability that had drawn her to him.

Nothing at all like the attractive, sophisticated and all-too-arrogant gentleman she had just encountered.

All in all, she preferred the awkward lad to the commanding earl, she told herself fiercely.

Coming to the outbuildings, Claire angled toward the plain stone manor house, where she was halted by the sight of a tall, slender woman with gray-streaked brown hair walking toward her. Not surprisingly Ann Stewart's shrewd gaze narrowed as it traveled over Claire's mud-stained hem and flushed features.

"Claire." A hint of disapproval marred the still-handsome features of the older woman. "Do not tell me that you have been to see Mr. Foster?"

Claire was immediately on the defensive. Although Ann Stewart was as close as any mother, there were times when they differed sharply.

Ann, the eldest daughter of the local vicar, had devoted her life to charitable works. She had provided an orphanage near the village that included a school, and become an advocate for the poor and elderly. She had also taken the motherless Claire under her wing and given the restless maiden a sense of meaning in her life.

But while Claire greatly admired her dear friend's serene strength and unwavering patience, she found her own impetuous nature rebelling in protest.

Where Ann would coax, Claire would demand. Where Ann would graciously accept fate, Claire would battle to the bitter end. Where Ann would walk around, Claire would plunge through. And where Ann would pray for the souls of men like Mr. Foster, Claire would threaten them with the magistrate.

Now she gave a small shrug. "Yes, I have been to see him."

"I specifically requested that you allow me to approach Mr. Foster," Ann remonstrated.

"You have already spoken with him. I thought I might have better luck."

Ann's expression became wry. "You mean you thought you could bully him into repairing the cottages."

"I thought he might be humiliated into repairing the cottages if he realized the entire neighborhood was aware of his shameful behavior," she corrected her friend.

"Mr. Foster possesses no shame."

Claire grimaced. "So I have discovered."

The thin features hardened. "What he does possess is a nasty temper, which is precisely why I did not wish for you to approach him on your own."

Claire shifted uneasily. She had no desire to discuss her encounter with Lord Challmond. Not when she was still attempting to recover her composure. But in such a small community there was little hope of keeping Lord Challmond and their fiery battle a secret. It would cause less speculation if she simply confessed the truth.

Or, at least, a portion of the truth.

"Actually I was not on my own."

Ann blinked in mild surprise. "No?"

"Lord Challmond has returned to Westwood Park."

"Has he?" Ann's expression softened with pleasure. "I had no notion he was coming to Devonshire."

Claire's own expression was far less pleased. "Neither did I."

"But this is wonderful."

Claire's deep blue eyes darkened unconsciously, a sure sign that her emotions were roused.

"I fail to comprehend what is so wonderful."

Ann regarded her young friend with growing curiosity. It was obvious she sensed that something had occurred.

"Lord Challmond is bound to replace Mr. Foster as soon as he realizes how shabbily he has managed the estate."

"Lord Challmond has displayed precious little interest in his estate in the past," Claire reminded the older woman. On how many occasions had the earl returned to Westwood, only to disappear after a fleeting visit with his elegant guests? The neighbors rarely even caught a glimpse of his elusive form before he was flitting back to London. Certainly he had never taken the time or the interest to ensure his tenants were being well treated. "What leads you to believe he shall take an interest now?"

"So he is not remaining?"

Claire gave a toss of her head. "I have not the least notion."

Ann's curiosity merely sharpened at Claire's fierce tone. "Has something occurred, Claire?"

Against her will Claire felt her cheeks bloom with color. She was not about to confess that Lord Challmond had stolen a kiss. Not to anyone. It was one of those things best forgotten.

"I do not know what you mean."

"You seem . . . flustered."

Claire forced a smile to her stiff lips. "Not at all."

Ann paused as she closely examined Claire's guarded expression, then, realizing she could not force a confidence from her young friend, she gave a small shrug.

"Well, at least while Lord Challmond is here we can ask for his donation to support the orphanage."

"Yes, I suppose."

A sudden glint entered Ann's blue eyes. "In fact, I will rely upon you to make the request, my dear."

"Me?" Claire gave a sharp shake of her head. "Oh, I think it would be best if you approached him, Ann."

"Nonsense. What gentleman can resist appearing at his most generous when a young, beautiful lady is making the request?" Ann lifted her brows. "Besides, I thought the two of you were old friends?"

"Hardly old friends," Claire instinctively denied. "He is, after all, considerably older than myself."

The brows arched even higher. "But you are better acquainted with him than I am."

"Truly, Ann, I would prefer—" Claire's hasty refusal was abruptly cut short as her father entered the courtyard. A slender gentleman with silver hair and blue eyes he was astonishingly attired in a brilliant green coat and yellow waistcoat. Accustomed to the tatty brown coats he had worn for years, Claire felt her mouth drop in surprise. "Oh, my."

Coming to a halt, Mr. Blakewell offered them a credible leg.

"Claire. Miss Stewart."

"Mr. Blakewell." Ann managed to smother her amusement at the transformation of her old friend.

"Father . . . are you going somewhere?"

"Yes, indeed." Henry Blakewell anxiously

patted his starched cravat. "How do you like my coat?"

"It is . . . most unusual. Where are you going?"

"I have promised Mrs. Mayer I would take her for a drive."

Claire could not have been more shocked if her father had announced he was going to toss himself off a nearby cliff. The scholarly gentleman rarely left his library for any reason, and certainly not to take any lady for a drive.

And Mrs. Mayer?

Claire shuddered. The woman was a—menace. Less than a year older than Claire's own two and twenty, Lizzy Hayden was the brash youngest daughter of a local merchant who had managed to ensnare a local squire. With her new position she had forced her way into the local drawing rooms. Then, swiftly nagging her husband to an early grave, the predatory widow began her hunt for a titled husband.

Any titled husband.

"Mrs. Mayer?" Claire demanded, certain that she must have misunderstood.

"A most charming lady." Her father glanced toward the startled Ann. "Do you not agree, Miss Stewart?"

"She is certainly"—Ann struggled to find an appropriate response—"a most resourceful young lady."

"A woman of character," Henry pronounced.

Ann coughed. "Yes, indeed."

Claire gave an impatient click of her tongue. "Why would you be taking Mrs. Mayer on a drive?" she demanded in her usual blunt manner.

"Why does any gentleman invite a lady for a drive?" Henry gave a shrug. "I wish to become better acquainted."

Claire gave a shake of her head. Was her father becoming a bit noddy? She remembered a great-aunt who had taken to running about without a stitch of clothing on when she grew old. Certainly that was no more queer than her father courting Lizzy Hayden.

"But why?"

"Really, my dear, that is rather a personal matter," her father retorted with a hint of censor in his tone. "I shall return later."

Offering a bow, Henry turned back to the waiting carriage. Claire watched his retreat with wide-eyed disbelief.

It was absurd.

"A drive with Mrs. Mayer?" she muttered.

Ann gave a low chuckle. "Well, well."

"What on earth is he up to?"

"My dearest, I should think that obvious."

"My father and Mrs. Mayer?" Claire gave a snort of disgust. "Absurd."

"Why?" Ann regarded her with a steady haze. "Your father is not infirm, and he has certainly been alone for a number of years. Why should he not seek companionship?"

Claire determinedly bit back the angry words that hovered on the tip of her tongue. Ann was no doubt merely teasing her. After all, they both knew Henry Blakewell possessed no interest in anything beyond his collection of rare manuscripts.

Still, it had been a trying day all around, and she was in little humor to find the notion of her father and the revolting Mrs. Mayer in any way amusing.

Giving a toss of her head, she swept past her friend toward the house.

"Absurd."

By the next morning Claire had managed to recover her temper, and ordering the large baskets of food from the kitchen to be loaded into her carriage, she set about her morning routine.

As always, she was sensibly attired in a sturdy russet gown and gold pelisse with heavy braiding that matched the trim on her bonnet. She paid little heed to fashion. It was far more important that she felt warm and comfortable. Especially on her morning visits to the nearby cottages.

Climbing onto the carriage, she took the reins of the matched grays and urged them out of the courtyard. Just for a moment she recalled Lord Challmond's stern warning at traveling about the countryside on her own. He had certainly proven how vulnerable she would be should she encounter a disreputable villain. Then she was sternly dismissing the ridiculous notion. She had driven and walked throughout the neighborhood for years without the least difficulty. The only danger she was in was from the annoying Lord Challmond.

With a determined expression she turned onto the narrow lane and wound through the fields. It was a fine morning, and soon Claire was pulling to a halt in front of a small cottage.

An air of neglect hung about the worn thatching and broken door, but Claire forced a smile as she collected a basket of food and entered the dark interior. As expected, she discovered a thin, fragile woman of indeterminate age lying upon a narrow bed. Claire's tender heart clenched at the weary pain lining the thin face.

The devil take Mr. Foster, she silently breathed.

"Ah, Miss Blakewell, so kind of you to come," Mrs. Foley breathed as she struggled to sit up.

"I have brought you some lovely soup and fresh bread," she said in bright tones.

The older woman gave a rattling cough. "So kind."

"Nonsense." Claire carefully unloaded the soup and bread onto a low table next to the bed, then moved to efficiently set a fire in the hearth. Even with the pale spring sunshine a chilled dampness filled the room. "I am pleased to help."

"You are a good lass. We are ever so grateful."

"I only wish I could do more."

"You have done more than anyone could ask."

The older woman's rattling cough made Claire wince.

"You are getting no better. It is this damnable cottage," she gritted out.

"I am sure that I am quite happy with the cottage, Miss Blakewell," Mrs. Foley fearfully retorted.

"Absurd. It is an insult to house anyone in such a dreadful place."

"Please, Miss Blakewell, do not say such things."

"Why not? It is no more than the truth."

"Yes, but . . . oh, my lord."

Dusting her hands, Claire abruptly turned around at Mrs. Foley's breathless greeting. Her own breath caught at the sight of Lord Challmond entering the cottage, his well-molded form consuming a disturbing amount of space.

Lifting a hand to her unruly heart, Claire refused to allow the handsome features and engaging green eyes to soften her disapproval.

Westwood Park was not in need of a charming rake. It needed an earl.

Easily reading the emotions flitting over her expressive countenance, Lord Challmond smiled wryly before turning back to his elderly tenant.

"No, do not get up, Mrs. Foley," he commanded as the old woman painfully scooted toward the edge of the bed. "How are you?"

"Fine," the widow blatantly lied. "Quite fine."

"Have you injured yourself?"

" 'Tis nothing."

"She is suffering from a weakness in her lungs that is aggravated by the dampness in this cottage," Claire promptly retorted.

"Oh, please, Miss Blakewell," Mrs. Foley protested in alarm. " 'Tis nothing."

"Lord Challmond should be made aware of the condition of his estate."

"Miss Blakewell is quite correct," Lord Challmond surprised them both by admitting as he stepped forward. "I fear I have been most neglectful in my duties." His gaze narrowed as it inspected the dark room. "I had no notion things had fallen into such disrepair."

Mrs. Foley gave a philosophical shrug of her shoulders.

"How could you know, when you be off fighting the French?"

"You are more forgiving than others, Mrs.

Foley," Lord Challmond retorted, deliberately glancing toward the frowning Claire.

"I t'ain't so old that I have forgot the frolics of youth, my lord." Mrs. Foley's expression was knowing.

"Thank you, but youth is no excuse for allowing my loyal tenants to be so shamefully treated." The dark countenance became suddenly somber. "I promise that things will soon improve."

The thin face flushed. After years of being bullied into submission by Foster, she was nearly overwhelmed by the earl's attention.

"Bless you."

"But first we shall have the apothecary tend to that cough."

"Oh, but there is no need."

"There is every need." That heart-jolting smile returned. "Indeed, you can consider it as my first command to you as your earl."

The older woman gave a dip of her head. "Very well, my lord."

"I shall leave you to enjoy your soup, but I will return later in the week."

With a brief, unreadable glance toward Claire, Lord Challmond turned and walked out of the cottage. Barely aware she was moving, Claire was swiftly in his wake. Once outside, she moved to where he was standing beside a magnificent stallion. As he turned to face her, she squarely met the emerald gaze.

"Thank you, my lord."

He gave a faint grimace. "There is no need to thank me, Miss Blakewell. As you so fiercely accused, it is my duty to care for Mrs. Foley as well as the rest of my tenants."

"Yes, but—" Claire cut her words abruptly short.

His gaze narrowed. "But what?"

"Nothing."

His full lips twisted with a sardonic amusement.

"Please do not spare my feelings now, Miss Blakewell."

Claire lifted her chin. If he wished the truth, then so be it.

"I did not think you would take the time to visit the cottages," she admitted.

The thin, aquiline nose flared as if she had managed to wound him.

"I suppose I deserve that," Lord Challmond muttered, then gave a sharp shake of his head. "But I am not the indifferent scoundrel you seem to consider me, Miss Blakewell. I would never have left Foster in control if I thought he would behave in such a reprehensible fashion." His brows lowered with a hint of impatience. "Why did no one contact me?"

"Who?" she demanded. "Your staff was terrified of Mr. Foster."

His frown only deepened. "I should have been informed."

Never one to mince her words regardless of

whom she was addressing, Claire placed her hands on her hips.

"You should have taken the trouble to discover for yourself, my lord."

The green eyes widened as if unaccustomed to being treated with such a blatant lack of toadeating. Then the sardonic smile returned.

"Touché," he murmured. "I should have." An odd, disturbing tremor inched down her spine. Something about the devilish gleam in his eye warned her of trouble. "Still, I am willing to admit when I am in the wrong."

"Good."

He stepped closer, his large frame almost touching her stiff body. Claire deeply inhaled the scent of his warm, clean skin.

"I am also determined to learn from my mistakes. You, however, are clearly stubborn to the point of foolishness."

Realizing that he was deliberately attempting to unnerve her, Claire forced herself to hold her ground.

"I beg your pardon?"

"I thought after yesterday you would have learned your lesson in tramping about unchaperoned."

A flare of heat darkened her ivory skin. "How dare you remind me of that—"

"Kiss?" he taunted.

"It is little wonder you are renowned as a rake, my lord," she accused him, wishing her voice did not sound so breathless. Still, she

took some consolation in the knowledge that
he would never know the endless hours she
had brooded over that brief kiss.

"If I were indeed a rake, I should not be
wasting our time alone with such a foolish ar-
gument." Without warning his slender hand
rose to cup her chin in a warm grasp. "Such
beautiful lips are meant to be enjoyed."

Claire gave a sharp gasp as his gaze dropped
to her mouth. Her lips parted, almost as if
inviting a kiss, and that tingling excitement
fluttered in the pit of her stomach.

No.

On this occasion she would not succumb to
the temptation of this charming scoundrel.

"Unhand me, my lord, or I shall bloody
your nose," she threatened between gritted
teeth.

A sudden, delighted laugh interrupted their
momentary privacy.

"Good God, Challmond, I do believe you
have at last met your match."

Three

Simon had left his estate early that morning with every intention of proving to himself that the lovely Miss Blakewell had been mistaken. Surely Foster could not be as bad as she had indicated? He would have known if something were amiss.

But it had taken only moments to realize that he was the one mistaken.

A smoldering fury lodged in the pit of his stomach as he visited the crumbling cottages and rode past the overgrown paddocks. Worse were the resigned faces of his tenants and their obvious disbelief in his promises to make things better.

It was no wonder Miss Blakewell charged him with neglect. The entire estate suffered beneath the care of Foster.

Of course, Foster's days at Westwood Park were done, he promised. He would personally run the villain off the estate. He would also ensure his next steward would be a man he could depend upon to care for Westwood Park when he was otherwise occupied.

Those had been the thoughts running through his mind when he had first entered Mrs. Foley's cottage. Then one glimpse of Miss Blakewell, and those thoughts had scattered.

Suddenly he was no longer aware of the neglected cottages and nagging guilt that he was avoiding his duties. Instead, he was remembering the feel of her slender body pressed close to his own and the delectable softness of her mouth. He had kissed dozens of women, most of whom were as experienced in the ways of pleasing a man as they were beautiful, but oddly, none had lingered in his thoughts in the manner this unruly, sharp-tongued shrew had managed to do. Indeed, the feel and taste of her had kept him awake long into the night.

And he had possessed every intention of kissing her once again when Locky had intruded upon their momentary privacy. Now he sternly smothered his flare of regret as he loosened his hold and stepped away.

"Ah, Locky, allow me to introduce Miss Blakewell. Miss Blakewell, my very great friend, Mr. Lockmeade."

Claire gave a small dip. "Mr. Lockmeade."

"Miss Blakewell." Locky closely surveyed Claire's fine features and stormy blue eyes as he bowed in return.

"Did you enjoy your walk?" Simon asked his friend.

The blunt features lit with genuine appreciation. "Yes, quite a nice bit of land you have here."

"So I am beginning to realize," Simon retorted in dry tones.

"I was on my way to the river." Locky paused as he eyed Simon in a speculative fashion. "I did not mean to intrude."

"You are not intruding," Claire denied in fierce tones, the charming color in her cheeks the only indication that she had been disturbed by his touch. "I did not realize Lord Challmond had a guest. Is this your first visit to Devonshire?"

"Yes."

"How nice. I am certain that once the neighborhood discovers that Lord Challmond is in residence, there will be any number of entertainments devised to keep you occupied."

Locky grimaced. "I fear I shall be more comfortable with the local trout than the local gentry."

Claire smiled with sympathetic humor, and suddenly Simon was struck with an absurd notion.

"Nonsense," he announced in decisive tones. "I shall introduce you to the neighborhood myself. We shall host a small gathering. Aunt Jane will no doubt agree to act as hostess. And, of course, Miss Blakewell will attend to ensure our success."

Even as the words left his mouth, he wondered at his own sanity. He had not come to

Devonshire to entertain. In fact, it had been his need to be away from society that had led him to Westwood Park. But somehow the thought of seeing Miss Blakewell seated at his table and playing his pianoforte was irresistible.

It was clearly not so irresistible to Miss Blakewell, who favored him with a glare.

"Unfortunately, Lord Challmond, I am much more like Mr. Lockmeade. I also prefer the trout to the gentry." With an effort she summoned a smile for Locky. "Please excuse me. I wish to ensure Mrs. Foley has eaten her soup."

Both gentlemen watched her stride briskly back into the cottage, then Locky turned to Simon with a mysterious smile.

"Spirited little thing."

Spirited, ill-mannered, and thoroughly adorable.

"Claire the Cat," he murmured with a low chuckle. "Come, Locky, we have a dinner to plan."

A week later Claire was seated in the library when her father entered, holding a gilt-edged card.

"A dinner party," he announced. "How delightful. I shall wear my new coat."

Claire blinked in surprise. When she had received the invitation to Lord Challmond's dinner party, she had simply tossed it onto the foyer table in annoyance. She had warned the arrogant lord she possessed no interest in his gathering. It had never occurred to her that her father would display the least interest in the invitation. Now she regarded him in disbelief.

"You plan to attend?"

"But of course." He appeared surprised by her question. "Why should I not attend?"

"You have always avoided such invitations," she retorted in exasperation. For goodness sake, what was the matter? It was bad enough that she was on edge because of Lord Challmond's disturbing presence in the neighborhood. Did she also have to worry that her father was losing his senses as well? "You claimed a rational gentleman preferred an evening with a good book and brandy to an evening with rattles and bores."

Henry smiled as he crossed the Brussels carpeting and stood next to the marble chimneypiece.

"That was before I became acquainted with Mrs. Mayer."

Claire gave a muffled choke of disbelief. "You must be jesting me."

"Not at all."

"But . . ."

"Yes?"

Claire hesitated. She had always been close to her father. Hardly surprising considering they had been on their own since her mother's death when she was just a child. And beyond their occasional disagreements over Claire's refusal to toss herself into the marriage mart, they had always rubbed along remarkably well. But suddenly she felt as if this man standing before her was becoming a stranger.

"You have never displayed the least interest in Mrs. Mayer," she pointed out as she set aside the book she had been reading. "Indeed, you have gone to considerable lengths to avoid her company."

Henry removed an enamel snuffbox from his pocket and delicately sniffed the scented tabac before responding.

"I have had a change of heart."

"But . . . why?"

He set the snuffbox on the mantel. "Because neither of us are getting any younger."

"What?"

He studied her puzzled expression for a moment, then slowly moved to settle himself next to her on the green and ivory striped sofa. Claire frowned at his strange behavior.

"I will admit that after your mother died I was content to withdraw from society. After all, I had you to bear me company, and I never intended to remarry."

Claire gave a slight shrug. "And?"

"And I was content with my life until the past few months."

Claire felt a sense of foreboding enter her heart. "What has occurred?"

"Nothing beyond the fact that I have grown to an age when I must consider the future." He paused and eyed her in a meaningful fashion. "Most important, the future of this estate once I am gone."

Gone? Was her father ill, she wondered with a stab of fear.

"That is ridiculous. You are far too young to consider such nonsense."

"Not if I desire to produce another heir."

Just for a moment Claire discovered it impossible to comprehend her father's meaning. After all, to produce another heir would mean having more children. And to have more children he would have to wed again. And he could not possibly contemplate such a farfetched notion.

Then something in his expression warned her that he was indeed referring to such a farfetched notion, and her fear catapulted to shock.

"Good God, Father, have you taken a blow to the head?"

"You need not appear so surprised," Henry chastised his daughter with a faint hint of pique. "As you said, I am not entirely ancient."

"Why would you wish for another heir?"

"Because, my dear, as much as I adore you, I have quite given up hope you will one day wed," he informed her in stern tones. "I want grandchildren who can keep the estate in the Blakewell family. So it has become obvious I shall have to wed again and hope for children that are more devoted to carrying on the family name than helping the needy."

Claire gave a slow shake of her head. Although her father had often chided her to travel to London for the Season, or to at least attend the local gatherings in search of a husband, he had never indicated he would go to these lengths for grandchildren. After all, the estate was not entailed. There was no fear it would be left to a distant relative who might force her out of her own home. And in truth, she had never considered what would happen after she was gone.

Suddenly, though, she realized that her father had not only considered the future but had decided to take matters into his own hands.

"But this is absurd," she exclaimed before she could halt the impetuous words. "You can not mean to marry Lizzy Hadford."

"Mrs. Mayer, my dear," her father corrected her.

Claire gave an impatient click of her tongue. "It does not matter what title she uses, she is still a common, fortune-seeking—"

"Claire, that is quite enough," Henry interrupted as he rose to his feet. "I will not hear another word against her."

"But—"

"I have made up my mind. Now I must prepare for the evening ahead."

With an uncharacteristically stubborn expression Henry Blakewell marched from the room and left behind a bewildered Claire.

Lizzy Hadford her stepmother?

That would mean that ghastly woman moving into Blakewell Manor. Claire would see her every day. She would be at the dining table every night. And in the breakfast room every morning and—

No.

Claire pressed a hand to her heaving stomach. It did not bear thinking of. But what could she do? Her father possessed every right to marry whomever he chose. Even if it was to a grasping harpy who would sell her own grandmother for a quid.

Moving toward the bay window that offered a view of the garden, Claire frantically attempted to think.

Her father obviously did not love Lizzy Hayden. What gentleman in his right mind could? His only interest was ensuring the future of the Blakewell estate. So, what she needed was a means of convincing him that the future of the estate was settled. At least until Lizzy had managed to lure another gullible fool to the altar. Perhaps then her father would at least choose a lady that was not thoroughly revolting.

But how?

For a long while Claire stared blindly out of the window, then a grim expression of determination settled on her delicate features.

She knew quite well that the only means she possessed of halting her father's ridiculous courtship was to begin one of her own.

Not a real courtship, she swiftly reassured herself. Not even to rid herself of Lizzy would she hand over her freedom to a husband. Her life was devoted to helping those in need, not pandering to the whims of a spoiled aristocrat. But there was nothing to halt her from pretending an interest in an eligible gentleman.

Once her father had become convinced he need not wed Lizzy, then Claire could return her life to normal.

Now all she needed was a gentleman willing to court her. . . .

Attired in a rich burgundy coat and silver pantaloons, Simon awaited his guests. A rather wry smile played about his mouth.

Over the past week he had debated several times on simply canceling the dinner party. Why would any gentleman of sense make such an effort to spend an evening with a lady? He had only to ride into the village to have any number of women make themselves available for his attentions.

But as he had passed the days attempting to

determine the vast repairs needed throughout his estate, he had discovered himself searching for a glimpse of Miss Blakewell. He had visited his tenants, attended the nearby church, and even ridden to Blakewell Manor on more than one occasion in the hope of encountering the elusive maiden, but she had maddeningly all but disappeared. And so the invitations to his dinner had duly been delivered, and he found himself actually looking forward to the evening ahead.

Surely Miss Blakewell would attend?

Simon poured himself a generous measure of brandy, then with a sense of relief watched as Locky entered the room. He was not certain he wished to dwell on his desire to be in the company of Miss Blakewell.

"Well, well . . . most elegant," he drawled as he regarded the black coat and white pantaloons.

Locky grimaced as he tugged at his knotted cravat. "I feel a fool."

Simon smiled in sympathy as he poured another measure of brandy. Poor Locky.

"Here." He crossed to place the glass in his friend's hand. "This shall soothe your discomfort."

Locky regarded him with a resigned amusement.

"I thought that we came to Devonshire for peace, not to prance about like the veriest dandies."

"It is a small gathering," Simon consoled. "Besides, as earl, it is expected I should contribute something to the neighborhood entertainments."

Locky's smile twisted. "Odd you did not speak of entertaining before you encountered Miss Blakewell."

"Did I not?" Simon blinked with seeming innocence.

"No."

"That is odd."

Locky gave a sudden chuckle. "She is very lovely."

Yes, she was lovely, Simon acknowledged with a stirring deep inside him. Perhaps the most lovely creature he had ever encountered.

"She also has the temper of a shrew and the tongue of a viper," he retorted. "A pity Prinny did not ship her to France when Napoleon first began creating difficulties. She would have frightened him into exile years ago."

Locky gave a shake of his head. "She cannot be so bad. She possesses the face of an angel."

"An angel? When we were children she terrified the entire neighborhood. I once watched her bully the local baker into climbing a tree to save a nest of baby birds after he killed the mother with a stone." He smiled at the memory. "She could not have been more than nine."

"Only a gentleman of considerable strength

could hope to manage such a woman," Locky murmured.

Simon instinctively stiffened. What the devil was Locky implying?

"Only a gentleman daft in the head would ever wish to manage such a woman."

Lifting his glass, Locky gave a faint shrug. "Perhaps."

Opening his mouth to argue further, Simon was halted as the butler entered the room to announce the arrival of his elderly aunt. With reluctance Simon swallowed his fierce words of denial. Locky was simply attempting to get a rise from him, he assured himself. Moving forward, he clasped the thin hand of the silver-haired woman.

"Ah, Aunt Jane, how lovely you look."

Jane gave a vague frown. "What?"

Simon leaned closer to speak directly in his relative's ear. Aunt Jane was notoriously hard of hearing, one of the reasons the previous earl had rarely invited her to Westwood Park, and it appeared her condition had only worsened.

"Lovely," he repeated loudly. "You look lovely."

"Oh . . . yes, quite nice weather." Aunt Jane smiled with benign goodwill.

Simon merely nodded his head. Aunt Jane meant well, and she was the only relative within the area who was in a position to act as his hostess. Leading her to the center of the room, Simon left her in the care of Locky as the butler returned with a short, jovial gentleman and his well-rounded wife.

"Lord and Lady Merfield," the servant announced.

Once again wondering at his own sanity, Simon moved to greet his guests. It was too late to regret the impulsive dinner invitations. He could only hope that it was worth his effort.

For the next half hour Simon was occupied with the elegant guests filling his drawing room. He set about charming his curious neighbors, although his gaze maintained a close guard on the doorway. His diligence was eventually rewarded as his butler entered with a gentleman attired in a shocking-red coat with pink pantaloons and following behind him the raven-haired beauty he had waited a week to see again.

"Mr. Blakewell and Miss Blakewell."

Simon stepped forward, his gaze lingering on the pale rose gown with silver netting that seemed to shimmer in the candlelight.

He was quite certain he had never seen a more beautiful woman.

With an effort Simon turned his attention back to the awaiting gentleman.

"Mr. Blakewell."

"My lord."

"I am very pleased you have come."

"Delighted," Henry retorted. "Simply delighted."

Simon smiled, then gratefully turned back to the silent maiden. Ignoring her frosty expression, he grasped her slender fingers and raised them to his lips. He felt a flare of satisfaction as she gave a faint shiver.

She was not as indifferent as she would have him believe.

"And the enchanting Miss Blakewell," he murmured softly. "I feared that you might not attend my modest gathering."

"How could I resist, my lord?" She firmly pulled her hand from his lingering grasp. "The neighborhood has been unable to speak of little else."

"I hope they shall not be disappointed."

"Yes, let us hope."

Simon laughed at her direct thrust. How refreshing she was from the horde of women who would agree with every word that passed his lips.

"You are quite exquisite."

The blue eyes darkened, but the frost never wavered.

"Must you flirt with every woman you encounter, my lord?"

"Despite your obvious belief, I am not a rake, Miss Blakewell," he assured her. "Indeed, I have been the bane of hopeful mamas who are in search for a suitable flirt for their daughters."

"Fah."

He laughed. "I see you are determined to

label me an incurable rogue. Perhaps we should discuss more important matters. I have not seen you at Mrs. Foley's. Have you stopped visiting her?"

As expected, a hint of embarrassment rippled over her countenance. Simon had no doubt that Claire had been avoiding the cottages in the fear he might appear. He also knew she would feel a measure of guilt at her absence.

"No, of course not. I went to see her this afternoon."

Knowing that he would be occupied, Simon acknowledged wryly.

"She is improved?"

"You know that she is, my lord."

"I have also ordered repairs at once on the cottages."

"Your tenants will be very pleased."

Barely aware that they were standing in a room filled with curious onlookers, Simon leaned even closer, inhaling deeply of the faint scent of lilacs.

"And what of you, Miss Blakewell?"

She eyed him in puzzlement. "Me?"

"Are you pleased?"

"Certainly."

"Good." Allowing his gaze to deliberately drop to the full softness of her mouth, Simon reluctantly stepped away. As much as he would have liked to devote the evening to the tantalizing Miss Blakewell, he had a duty to his guests. "I believe dinner is about to be served. Excuse me."

Four

Blast, blast, and blast.

With a rising sense of exasperation Claire glanced about the drawing room. Who would have thought that carrying out her secret campaign would be so difficult?

Had she not taken special care to choose her most elegant gown and even had allowed her maid to smooth her hair into a tidy knot with delicate curls left to frame her face? And had she not tossed aside all reason and determinedly set about charming the numerous eligible gentlemen in attendance?

But oddly she had discovered her efforts had produced precious few results. Indeed, every gentleman whom she approached regarded her with varying degrees of suspicion and even downright apprehension. For goodness' sake, one would think they were actually terrified of her, she thought with a flare of disgust.

Her restless gaze eventually halted on the thin, pasty-faced gentleman currently attempting to hide behind a large marble urn. A twinge of reluctance tugged at her heart.

Mr. Limpet was a timid, awkward young man who devoted his life to his overbearing mother. He rarely spoke a word in company and never to an unmarried female. It would be a difficult task to lure him into a flirtation.

For a moment she hesitated, then, turning her head, she caught a glimpse of Mrs. Mayer clasped onto her father's arm with a relentless determination. Claire's gaze narrowed at the plunging neckline and sheer material of the brilliant scarlet gown. The woman was barely decent, she seethed. Not that her smitten father appeared to mind her lack of modesty. He had not taken his eyes off those overly exposed charms all evening.

There seemed nothing for it, she acknowledged. It would have to be Mr. Limpet.

With an expression that sent guests scurrying out of her determined path, Claire made her way across the drawing room to her unknowing prey. As she neared, Mr. Limpet hastily turned to gape at the fine watercolor hanging on the wall. He clearly hoped she would walk on past. Coming to a halt, she summoned what she hoped was a seductive smile.

"A beautiful painting, do you not agree, Mr. Limpet?" she inquired sweetly.

With a tiny jolt Mr. Limpet turned to blink at her in a nervous manner.

"Oh . . . I . . ." He cleared his throat. "Yes, if you think it is lovely, Miss Blakewell."

Claire firmly attempted to ignore the pale, protruding eyes and rather unfortunate stench of an unwashed body.

"I fear I haven't much artistic talent." She paused, then, when it was obvious Mr. Limpet was merely going to blink at her, she continued. "Do you paint?"

"Oh . . . no, I fear not."

"But you must have other talents?"

He paused as if he were considering bolting for freedom, then, clearly realizing she had him cornered, he nervously shifted his feet.

"I . . . collect things."

"Indeed?" Claire forced a note of interest in her voice. "And what things do you collect?"

"Insects."

Claire frowned, quite certain she must have misunderstood.

"Insects?"

"Dead ones, you know. I put them in pots and jars to study."

"How . . . intriguing." Claire suppressed a shudder. Dead bugs? Good God. Still, bugs, dead or not, were preferable to Lizzy. "I have never seen an insect collection. Perhaps you would show them to me?"

"You wish to see them?" he stuttered.

"Certainly."

"Oh. I do not know—"

"Surely you wish to share your collection with others?"

"I . . . suppose."

"Perhaps you could come to dinner one evening? I am certain Father would wish to see your bugs as well."

"Dinner?" he squeaked.

"You do eat, do you not?"

"Not . . . that is . . ."

"Would Friday suit you?" Claire persisted determinedly.

"I . . . um . . ." The protruding eyes bulged even farther, then Mr. Limpet's nerve broke altogether and he stumbled backward. "I believe Mama is in need of me."

Knocking over a small table, Mr. Limpet forged a path around Claire and with obvious relief scurried to the safety of his mother's side. Left on her own, Claire swallowed a sigh of exasperation.

Really. What was she doing wrong?

She had seen a dozen ladies who had only to smile to have a bevy of moonstruck gentlemen swarm to their side. But while she had gone out of her way to be charming, all she had received were startled apologies and swift retreats.

Granted she possessed little experience with gentlemen and flirtations, but she was well enough acquainted with the process to realize that her intended prey should not be fleeing in terror.

Perhaps she should have taken more time

to learn how to emit shrill giggles and bat her eyes in a foolish manner, she told herself dryly.

Decidedly piqued, Claire was unaware of the gentleman closely regarding her every movement. In truth, it came as a distinct shock when the familiar male cologne warned her that she was no longer alone. Glancing up, she discovered Lord Challmond standing close at her side. Her heart gave a queer jolt of alarm.

"Miss Blakewell," he murmured, an odd glint in the emerald eyes.

"My lord."

"Are you enjoying your evening?"

"It has been . . . pleasant," she forced herself to lie. She could hardly admit that it had been a dismal failure since she had been unable to lure a susceptible gentleman into her charade.

"Yes." His smile held a hint of devilment. "I believe the pheasant was a trifle overdone and the wine a bit young, but overall I am quite pleased."

"How fortunate."

"I must say, however, that I am somewhat perplexed by one thing, Miss Blakewell."

"Oh?" A wary expression settled on her pale countenance. She did not like that smile. "And what is that, my lord?"

"The reason you are terrifying my gentlemen guests."

She felt the color drain from her face in

horror. He could not possibly have realized what she was doing.

Could he?

"I beg your pardon?"

His arms folded over the width of his chest, his gaze taking careful note of the tension stiffening her slender body.

"I have watched, with some enjoyment I might add, as you have stalked and cornered every eligible gentleman available this evening excepting myself and Locky, until you have sent them scurrying in terror."

Why the—rat, she seethed in humiliation. He had obviously been spying on her the entire evening.

"That is preposterous," she attempted to bluff.

His smile merely widened. "At first I presumed you were hounding the poor blokes for your latest cause. After all, a young buck cannot wish to share his allowance on orphanages and schools or to fill his estate with stray curs. But then I noted the hint of panic in their eyes. They looked very much like fresh recruits seeing their first battle." He paused, the emerald eyes dancing. "Or an unfortunate chap being pursued by a marriage-mad female."

The color rushed back to her face with a vengeance. The devil take the annoying lord. Did he not have more important matters beyond herself to occupy his mind?

"Should you not be tending to your guests, my lord?" she gritted out.

He leaned closer, the heat and scent of him wrapping about her.

"Is that it, Miss Blakewell? Are you on the hunt for a husband?"

"Certainly not." Her eyes darkened with annoyance. "A lady would have to be without sense to burden herself with a husband. I wish to achieve far more than running a comfortable household and producing heirs."

There was no mistaking the sincerity in her tone, and an unreadable expression flickered over his handsome countenance.

"Indeed? Then, what is your interest in these gentlemen?"

"I was simply being polite."

Intent on each other, neither noticed the large, florid-faced woman bearing down on them with the determination of Wellington's forces.

"Ah, Miss Blakewell," Mrs. Limpet boomed without apology for her intrusion. "My son informs me that you are interested in viewing his insects. I have told him to bring them to you tomorrow."

Claire swallowed her instinctive refusal. Had she not wanted her father to believe she was interested in Mr. Limpet? What did it matter if she found Mr. Limpet repulsive and his mother a bully? Or that Lord Challmond was regarding her with open amusement?

"Thank you, Mrs. Limpet. I shall look forward to viewing his collection."

With a regal nod of her head Mrs. Limpet swept back toward her cringing son. Once again alone with Lord Challmond, Claire lifted her reluctant gaze to meet his amused expression.

"What?" she challenged.

"Insects?"

"Mr. Limpet collects them."

"And you are interested in insects?" he mocked.

"They can be quite fascinating."

"Oh, I am certain." His low chuckle seemed to tingle down her spine. "But not nearly as fascinating as you, Miss Blakewell."

He intently studied her upturned countenance, as if seeking the answer to her odd behavior. Claire discovered herself struggling to maintain her composure beneath his scrutiny.

"I should find my father. He will be wishing to leave soon."

With a deliberate motion Lord Challmond turned to where Mr. Blakewell was chatting in an intimate fashion with Mrs. Mayer.

"Your father appears quite content."

Claire grimaced. "He is clearly unaware of the time."

"What is time to a gentleman enjoying the delights of a beautiful woman?"

"That is not amusing, my lord. Please excuse me."

Having endured enough of Mrs. Mayer, Mr. Limpet, and certainly Lord Challmond, Claire flashed Simon a warning frown before sweeping around his towering form and toward her father. This disastrous evening was entirely Henry Blakewell's fault, she thought with a flare of annoyance. Him and his absurd notion to remarry. Coming to a halt at his side, Claire regarded him in a stern manner.

"Father, should we not be on our way?"

Henry frowned at her abrupt tone. "Claire, you have not even greeted Mrs. Mayer."

With reluctance Claire shifted to meet the simpering smile of the widow Mayer.

"Lizzy."

"Sweet Claire," the woman cooed. "How charming you look this evening. I never noticed how closely you resemble your handsome father."

"Fustian." Claire gave a loud snort. "As everyone knows, I have always resembled my mother."

"Claire," her father chastised in disapproving tones, "perhaps you are correct, we should be on our way."

Indifferent to Claire's obvious dislike, Lizzy laid a hand upon Henry's arm.

"I will see you tomorrow?"

"Certainly," Henry promised, ignoring his daughter's narrowed gaze.

With a bow Henry made his way to Lord Challmond to make their farewells, then, returning to Claire, he led her to the foyer. There was a brief wait as their carriage was called, and in silence they allowed the footman to hand them into the leather seats. Only when they were traveling down the path to Blakewell Manor did her father bring her to task for her ill-mannered behavior.

"There is no need to be rude to Mrs. Mayer."

Claire shivered at the chilled night air. "Was I rude?"

"You know quite well that you were."

"I merely pointed out my resemblance to my mother. You are always commenting on how like her I am."

"You were attempting to make her feel uncomfortable."

"Trust me, Father, nothing could make that woman feel uncomfortable."

There was a slight pause before her father shifted the conversation to a more pleasant subject.

"Well, at least you managed to be charming to one person this evening."

Claire felt a faint flare of hope. So her father had noticed her efforts after all.

"Yes?"

"I must say the gentleman was very, very taken with you. He could not take his gaze off you the entire evening."

Claire could only presume it was a father's hope that made him exaggerate in such a fashion. Mr. Limpet had devoted the better part of the evening staring at his own toes.

"Indeed?"

"I should not at all be surprised if you can number him among your admirers quite soon."

"Well, Mr. Limpet is very kind," she murmured.

"Mr. Limpet? I was not referring to Mr. Limpet."

"No?"

Her father gave a click of his tongue. "I am not so birdwitted as to presume you would be interested in that looby. I was speaking of Lord Challmond."

Claire's heart gave a queer flop that had nothing to do with the sudden curve they were rounding.

"Lord Challmond?"

"A most eligible gentleman."

"Lord Challmond?" she repeated in disbelief.

"Charming, intelligent, and of impeccable birth," her father continued, a note of satisfaction laced though his voice, almost as if he were listing the merits of a favorite stallion. "Yes, a young lady would be extremely fortunate to capture the attentions of Lord Challmond."

"She would be dicked in the nob if you ask me," Claire muttered beneath her breath.

"What, my dear?"

Claire leaned her weary head against the leather squabs.

"Nothing, Father."

"As you see, this is the common roach."

Claire's stomach rolled in protest as Mr. Limpet held out a small bottle emitting a peculiar odor. Although she had never considered herself particularly squeamish, Claire found it increasingly difficult to maintain an air of polite interest as her guest pulled out one bottle after another.

Who would have imagined one person could have collected so many bugs?

"Ah . . . fascinating," she forced herself to murmur.

Blast, she had been a fool to pretend an interest in such a distasteful hobby.

Mr. Limpet waved the bottle beneath her nose. "Would you like to hold it?"

"No." She struggled to temper her sharp tone. "No, thank you."

"Come, Miss Blakewell," a dark voice drawled from the open French windows. "I thought you found insects fascinating?"

Claire felt her heart clench in dismay as she abruptly turned to view the tall, auburn-haired gentleman nonchalantly stepping into the room. Drat the man. How did he always manage to appear when he was least welcome?

"Lord Challmond," she acknowledged.

Lord Challmond offered a graceful leg. "Good morning, Limpet. Miss Blakewell."

"Lord Challmond." Mr. Limpet awkwardly rose to his feet.

"I see that you are sharing your collection with Miss Blakewell."

Limpet coughed, pulling at his cravat. "I . . . ah . . . yes."

Lord Challmond turned to Claire with a bland smile. "You are fortunate, indeed, Miss Blakewell."

She narrowed her gaze in frustration. Did the gentleman have nothing better to do than annoy her?

"Yes, we were quite enjoying our morning," she retorted pointedly.

His smile widened. "What lady would not enjoy being tutored in the mysteries of insects?"

Thoroughly unaware of the amusement smoldering just below Lord Challmond's smooth composure, Mr. Limpet gave a startled blink.

"Are you interested in insects, my lord?"

"Unfortunately my knowledge of insects is sadly lacking."

"That is unfortunate." Claire flashed a sudden smile. "I am certain that Mr. Limpet would be pleased to instruct you, my lord. Would you not, Mr. Limpet? Perhaps later this afternoon?"

"Oh, yes . . . delighted." Mr. Limpet beamed in a pleased fashion.

Lord Challmond flashed Claire a wryly appreciative glance. "Perhaps at a later date."

"Certainly." Mr. Limpet gave a startled exclamation as he caught sight of the gilt-bronze mantel clock. With hurried movements he set about returning the bottles to his leather case. "I fear I must return to Mother."

"So soon?" Claire demanded, conveniently forgetting her earlier wish for Mr. Limpet to go far, far away and take his nasty bugs with him. Bugs were a small price to pay not to be left on her own with Lord Challmond.

Mr. Limpet did not even pause as he buckled the case shut.

"Mother does not wish me to leave her beyond an hour. Her nerves are not at all well."

"She is fortunate to possess such a dedicated son," Lord Challmond congratulated Mr. Limpet, his gaze never leaving Claire's pale countenance.

"Yes." Mr. Limpet offered a swift bow. "Good day."

Claire watched in silence as Mr. Limpet hurried from the room, bumping into a chair and nearly upsetting a French oval table prettily inset with a Sèvres porcelain plaque. How had she ever thought to fool her father into believing she could be interested in such a man? she wondered with a sigh. Then, turning to her unwelcome intruder, she eyed him squarely.

"Is there something that you need, my lord?"

He shrugged, appearing absurdly handsome in his avocado coat and buff breeches.

"I had thought since you have developed such a fascination with insects, you might enjoy a ride. We can find any number of roaches and spiders in the far meadows."

Her smile was without humor. "As tempting as it might be, my lord, I fear that I must decline—"

Her determined refusal was interrupted as her father stepped into the room and came to a sudden halt at the sight of Lord Challmond.

"I did not realize we had a visitor."

Lord Challmond gave a bow, not bothering to apologize for his unorthodox intrusion into the manor.

"Mr. Blakewell."

"Lord Challmond." The older gentleman turned toward his daughter. "I was on my way to Mrs. Mayer's. I thought perhaps you would join me? It would be the perfect opportunity for the two of you to become better acquainted."

A flare of panic raced through Claire. Spend the day with Lizzy? Good God, was it not enough she had endured the morning with Mr. Limpet and his bugs?

No, she simply could not bear it.

Claire turned toward the tall form of Lord

Challmond. A startling, nearly unbelievable notion bloomed in her mind.

Her father already believed she was interested in this gentleman. He had in fact given his blessing to a relationship between the two of them the night before. Could she possibly endure Lord Challmond's aggravating presence long enough to convince her father he had no need of Lizzy Hayden?

A shiver of alarm raced through her body, but Claire sternly ignored the warning. Nothing, absolutely nothing, could be worse than Lizzy as her stepmother.

"That would be delightful, Father. Unfortunately I have just promised Lord Challmond I would ride with him this morning."

Five

Simon was decidedly intrigued. He was well aware the chit was up to some devious scheme. After all, she openly professed a staunch distaste for the bonds of matrimony. And yet throughout the party she behaved as any other maiden on the prowl for a prospective husband.

Well, perhaps not like every other maiden, he amended with a flare of amusement. There were not many other maidens with her beauty and wealth that would send an entire roomful of gentlemen fleeing in terror. Lord, he had nearly laughed aloud to watch the young men blanch at her awkward flirtations.

And so he had ridden over that morning, determined to discover the truth behind her odd behavior, only to be thrown off guard by her abrupt agreement to go for a ride. He had been thoroughly expecting to have to browbeat her into accompanying him. Or even having to resort to actual kidnapping. To have her so easily comply sent a rash of suspicion through his mind.

Glancing sideways, Simon covertly studied the delicate profile of the woman seated at his side. Attired in a pink gown with a deep rose spencer, she was breathtakingly lovely. So lovely, he felt his heart give an odd twinge. Suddenly he was delighted he had brought his groom to drive so that he could concentrate on the mysterious maiden rather than on the spirited grays pulling the open carriage.

With an effort he reined in his wayward thoughts and instead concentrated on the puzzle of Miss Blakewell.

"I find myself bewildered once again, Miss Blakewell." He finally broke the silence of the early spring.

With a decidedly wary expression she turned to meet his probing gaze.

"Pardon me?"

"Are you going to confess why you suddenly agreed to join me this morning?"

She gave a vague shrug. "I simply had a change of heart."

"A change of heart?"

"Is that so surprising?"

"With you nothing is surprising. Still, I find it distinctly intriguing. I am not so much a looby as to flatter myself that your change of heart was influenced by my charms."

"Perhaps I merely wished to enjoy the fine weather."

He gave a sharp laugh. "You will have to do better than that, Miss Blakewell."

"Can we please discuss something else, my lord?" she retorted pertly. "I find the subject giving me a headache."

His lips quirked. Vixen. He would clearly have to be more subtle in his approach.

"We cannot have that. Allow me instead to inquire as to why you have never traveled to London."

She blinked in bewilderment at the abrupt question. "For a season, you mean?"

"Yes."

"I told you, I possess no interest in attracting a husband."

He tilted his auburn head to one side. "There are other attractions beyond the marriage mart in London," he pointed out. "Museums, the theater, concerts."

"I have been far too occupied to leave Devonshire."

Simon paused. He could not think of one lady who could resist the temptations of glittering London society. Especially a lady who could easily have claimed the title of an Incomparable.

"Occupied with what?" His gaze suddenly narrowed. "Or should I say whom?"

"Miss Stewart, of course," she retorted as if he were a fool to even ask.

"The vicar's daughter?"

Without warning, the blue eyes flared with an inner fire. Her vivid beauty was more pronounced than ever.

"She has accomplished the most amazing things." Claire seemed to forget momentarily her prickly dislike toward him as she spoke of her friend. "In just the past ten years she has established an orphanage with a wonderful school and a charity that supports workers who were injured in the factory."

Simon was only vaguely acquainted with Miss Stewart. He recalled a calm, rather quiet lady with a pleasing smile. Certainly nothing at all like the spirited hellion at his side. Still, Claire's admiration for Miss Stewart and her accomplishments were unmistakable.

"Quite impressive."

"She is the only truly good person I know," Miss Blakewell continued, as if to impress upon Simon the saintliness of Miss Stewart. "She is kind and generous and always patient. My one wish in life is to follow in her example by devoting my life to helping others. There could be nothing more rewarding."

Not nearly as saintly as the vicar's daughter, Simon felt a flare of distaste. It was one thing to champion the cause of the defenseless. Or to help those in need. Such characteristics were as much a part of Claire Blakewell as her sharp tongue and fiery temper. But to think of her sacrificing her entire life to others was oddly unwelcome.

"You cannot mean to devote all of your time to charitable works?" he protested.

"Certainly I do." Her chin jutted out in a

growingly familiar motion. "And I hope that someday Miss Stewart and I can travel to other places throughout England and even the Continent to establish similar schools."

Simon swallowed his instinctive urge to protest such an absurd scheme. As much as he might dislike the notion of Claire becoming an old spinster as she toiled for others, he was wise enough to realize the least hint of reproach would only ensure her folly.

"A very noble cause," he forced himself to say.

Her chin inched higher. "Yes, it is."

"A rather lonely future, however."

She shrugged. "It is what I prefer."

This beautiful woman alone? Ludicrous.

"You are very close to Miss Stewart," he said.

"Yes." Her expression softened. "After my mother died, she began to invite me to the vicarage. No doubt my father hoped she would influence me to become a proper lady. Instead, she inspired me to join in her cause to help others."

His auburn brows lifted. "So you are attempting to mold yourself in the image of Miss Stewart?"

She eyed him squarely. "What are you implying?"

He smiled in a rueful fashion. He had to admit he found it decidedly peculiar that both he and Claire would have been influenced by someone other than their parents, but while she was clearly determined to become another Ann Stewart, he had fled with all speed from the Earl of Challmond.

"Nothing at all."

She eyed him with suspicion. "I should be very pleased to be compared to Miss Stewart."

"Indeed." His tone was deliberately mild. It was too beautiful a day to argue. Especially with the delectable vixen. "I intend to call on her later in the week."

"Really?"

"I hoped that she will be able to suggest a competent replacement for Foster."

She did not bother to hide her surprise. "Foster is gone?"

Simon grimaced as he recalled the beastly scene with his steward. The blackguard had shrilly denied pocketing the allowance meant for the estate upkeep; he had even implied that the tenants themselves were responsible for their miserable conditions. But once realizing that Simon would not be swayed, he revealed an ugly, vindictive nature that had revolted the earl. How could he ever have left his people in the care of such a brute?

"I have given him a fortnight to leave the estate, although I have relieved him of all duties."

"Oh."

His expression lightened. "You appear surprised?"

"Perhaps a bit."

"Pleasantly surprised, I hope?" he demanded, surprised himself by the knowledge that he wished to please this woman.

"Of course," she retorted. "Foster was an incompetent bully."

He couldn't prevent a laugh at her blunt reproach. She was nothing if not brutally honest.

"Be assured that my next steward shall be fully aware of my expectations, especially in regard to my tenants."

Just for a moment the blue eyes appeared to darken.

"So you intend to leave?"

Did he? Simon discovered himself shying from the question.

"I am uncertain what I intend to do." His lips twisted. "Odd, is it not?"

"What do you mean?"

"Since I was born I have had others planning my future. My parents, Lord Challmond, my headmasters, and finally Wellington. Now that I am in the position to make my own choices I seem remarkably unable to do so."

Once again she did not bother to soften her words. "Westwood Park needs an earl, my lord."

Simon winced before giving a resigned chuckle. "As you say, my little cat."

A short silence fell as they turned onto a narrow path that led through the rolling meadow. A flood of pale sunlight danced over the countryside, adding a hint of welcome warmth.

Inwardly Simon pondered her sharp words. Westwood Park did need an earl. His brief inspection of his lands had effectively proven that. And he could not deny that a part of him still felt an attachment to the estate. More than once he had caught himself pondering how best to rotate a field or repair a barn. Thoughts that were as unnerving as they were unexpected.

Granted, he had always known that he would take control of Westwood Park. It had been his destiny since the previous Lord Challmond had failed to produce the necessary heir. And, of course, it had been firmly reinforced when that Lord Challmond had arrived at his moher's door with a large bank draft to allow the next heir to be raised at Westwood Park. The money had been badly needed for the struggling widow, who had readily handed Simon over.

But the thought of shouldering the dull responsibilities of a proper landlord made him shudder. Was he prepared to become the stern, humorless Earl of Challmond? Did he truly wish to spend his days hunched over the accounting books or settling the complaints of his tenants? Could he give up his carefree existence?

For no reason he could comprehend, his

gaze shifted to linger on the pale countenance of Miss Blakewell. He had to admit a gentleman would never become dull or grim-faced with this firebrand about.

At last the carriage rolled to a halt at the edge of a copse of trees. With a small smile he met his companion's wary glance.

"Why have we halted?"

"I thought you would enjoy a short stroll," he retorted, climbing out of the carriage and holding out an imperative hand. "Come."

She hesitated, as if considering denying his request, then clearly deciding that it was not worth the fuss, she placed her hand in his.

"Very well."

With care he helped her to alight, then, ignoring the tightening of her lips, he firmly tugged her arm through his own. Quite deliberately he led her deeper into the shaded glade, moving toward the nearby stream. Claire appeared to be unaware she was being carefully herded, until they rounded a large bush to discover an elegant picnic spread upon the mossy ground.

Simon noted the amazed disbelief that rippled over Claire's face with a sense of satisfaction. He had taken great pains to ensure she would be suitably impressed, and his servants had not disappointed him.

A large cover was nicely arranged among the dappled sunlight, laden with elegant trays of trout, pheasant, delicate pastries, and strawberries fresh from the hothouse. He had requested the finest Wedgwood dishes and crystal glasses for the chilled champagne. Surrounding all were lavish bouquets of red roses that provided an exotic spice to the air. Then, at his signal, the soft sounds of a violin from behind another bush floated through the trees.

"Oh . . ." Claire, perhaps for the first time in her young life, appeared at a loss for words.

Simon gave a pleased chuckle before turning to the uniformed butler standing a discreet distance away.

"Thank you, Calvert, it appears perfect."

Calvert gave a slight bow. "Thank you, my lord."

"I . . . what is this?" Claire demanded.

"A picnic."

She gave a shake of her head, far from satisfied by his bland response.

"But . . . how did you know I would agree to join you for a drive?"

He held her gaze as he slowly lifted her hand to his lips.

"I possess unwavering faith in my powers of persuasion."

He felt her tremble before she was firmly tugging her fingers free.

"Fah."

"Allow me." Gently clasping her elbow, he tugged her through the roses to place her on the cover. Then, still using her obvious bewilderment, he filled a plate with the waiting delicacies. "You see, I have not forgotten your weakness for strawberries." He settled beside her, pressing a large berry between her lips. "Delectable."

Instinctively she ate the strawberry, licking the juice from her lips in an unconsciously provocative motion.

"Lord Challmond."

"Yes, Miss Blakewell?"

"This is very nice, but I . . . I should be returning home."

Simon poured them both a glass of champagne, offering her the crystal flute with a chiding grin.

"Surely you cannot mean to offend my cook, Miss Blakewell?" he protested. "Just consider the effort she has gone to."

Her gaze narrowed. "That is not fair."

"Perhaps not, but true nevertheless." He tilted his head to one side. "You will stay?"

"Very well," she conceded grudgingly.

Simon laughed, filling his own plate. He could name a dozen, perhaps even several dozen maidens who would have swooned with delight at the romantic picnic. It was an elegant feast designed to seduce the senses. The faint strains of Mozart, the scent of roses, the exquisite meal, and soft breeze that danced through the trees. A susceptible maiden should have been swept off her feet, but Miss

Blakewell merely nibbled on her food, a guarded expression on her face.

Still, he thought with a flare of wry amusement, at least she had not stormed off in a fury or blackened his eye at his audacity. Perhaps age had tempered her hellion spirit a bit.

But just a bit.

At last sensing his intense scrutiny of her profile, Claire turned to regard him with a frown.

"What?"

He absently nibbled on the sliced pheasant. "I am merely recalling you as a grubby schoolgirl."

She gave a shrug. "You were occasionally grubby yourself."

"Do you recall when Froggy dared you to spend the night in the old abbey?"

Claire wrinkled her nose at the memory of the pudgy, ill-natured son of a local viscount. Although he had been a spiteful bully, Simon had always suspected the cad had nurtured a violent attraction for Claire.

"He was a pest."

"He also knew you were terrified of the dark," Simon retorted. "Not that you would back down from his dare."

"I would never have remained if you had not arrived," she admitted.

"I could not allow you to lose a bet," Simon said, not willing to confess he had followed her out of a fear that Froggy would seek her out at the isolated abbey. Older than Claire, he was all too aware of the dangers of a young girl on her own. And a portion of him had suspected the cunning Froggy had simply desired a chance to force his attentions on the innocent child. So he had slipped from his chamber and followed Claire to the abbey, where he had remained on full alert for the course of the long night. "Not when you had pushed him into the pond for daring to mock my decidedly large ears. Whatever happened to dear Froggy?"

"He was forced to marry his cousin after he lost his inheritance at the gaming tables."

The image of a gaunt, sour-faced woman several years his senior rose to mind.

"Not Daisy?"

"Yes."

"Egad, poor blighter." He gave a dramatic shudder. "Not even Froggy deserved such a ghastly fate."

A reluctant smile tugged at her full lips. "I do not feel sympathy for him. He was a horrid sneak."

Simon was swift to take advantage of her softened disposition. Setting aside his plate, he scooted close enough to smell the scent of lilacs.

"Perhaps, but I wish he were near," he murmured.

She blinked in surprise. "Good Lord, why?"

"I would not object if he were to once again

dare you to spend the night at the abbey." His voice dropped to a husky pitch. "An evening together would be far more intriguing now."

Her soft lips parted in shock. "My lord."

"I was once Simon."

She hastily set aside her plate and champagne, a hint of panic darkening her blue eyes.

"My lord, we should be returning."

"There is no hurry." His glance shifted toward her abandoned plate. "You have not finished your strawberries."

"I am quite finished."

Simon lifted a slender hand, and immediately the butler was at his side.

"Calvert, you may pack this away."

"Very good, my lord."

Appearing as if he were in the finest dining room, Calvert efficiently packed the platters into a basket before returning for the plates and crystal. Then, with a discretion that Simon could only appreciate, he returned to the carriage nearly hidden behind a distant bush.

Not nearly as pleased with the turn of events as Simon, Claire shifted uneasily.

"Are we not leaving?"

"As I said, there is no hurry." His hand slowly rose to tug the ribbons of her bonnet. Before she could protest, he had plucked the satin concoction from her dark curls and tossed it onto the blanket. "Do you recall how

I held you in my arms during our night together?"

A flood of color warmed her cheeks. "I recall very little, sir. I was barely twelve."

His gaze dropped to her enticing mouth as he leaned forward.

"Shall I refresh your memory?"

"Lord Challmond . . . Simon," she protested, her hands rising to press against his chest.

He felt an unfamiliar warmth burst through his heart. "I like the sound of my name upon your lips," he breathed. Gads, this woman was a desirable minx!

Her eyes dark with emotion, she sucked in a sharp breath. A delectable pulse leapt at the edge of her mouth, revealing that she was far from indifferent to his nearness.

"Stop this foolishness at once," she commanded in a breathy voice.

"But why?" His hand moved to stroke her satin-smooth cheek. "Such . . . foolishness can be a delightful means of passing a spring day."

For a moment her lips parted, almost as if in invitation, then, seeming to gather her senses, she abruptly stiffened.

"I have already warned you, my lord."

"Ah, yes, that you would bloody my nose."

"Yes," she gritted out.

His eyes danced with wicked pleasure. "Perhaps it would be worth a bloody nose or two."

"Oh . . ."

Her protest was cut short as he claimed her mouth in a possessive kiss. For a moment she stiffened, then her lips melted beneath his demand and he could taste the lingering sweetness of strawberries. Simon moaned in satisfaction, gathering her close to his chest. It had been far too long since their last kiss, he thought as his pulse quickened. Odd, considering that he never longed for the practiced seduction of his various mistresses with such intensity. Why Claire's seductive innocence would prove so enticing was a thought he refused to dwell upon.

Feeling the heat surge through his body, Simon deepened the kiss, then, with a restless need, he trailed his mouth over the line of her jaw and down the soft curve of her neck.

Damn, but this woman stirred his passions.

Lost in the mounting sensations, Simon barely noted the distant shout or the sudden cry that echoed through the trees. Indeed, his only thought was to continue the delightful task of nibbling the satin skin of her neck, when Claire abruptly pulled away.

"Oh . . ." she said for the second time.

"Oh, indeed," Simon murmured, preparing to claim her lips in another kiss, when her hands firmly pushed against his chest.

"Simon, halt that," she insisted, struggling to her feet despite his protest. "We must help that poor little boy."

Six

Finding it ridiculously difficult to keep her knees from buckling, Claire attempted to concentrate on the ragtag boy struggling to free himself from the grip of the grim-faced butler.

La, what was the matter with her, she wondered in disbelief.

The gentleman was a shameless seducer. What other reason could there be for his lavish picnic and well-practiced kisses?

But like the most susceptible simpleton, Claire had been unable to resist the temptation. There had been something enticing in the thought of a gentleman going to such an effort for her pleasure. And as far as his kisses . . . well, there was little point in denying that they created the most delicious sensations. Or that she had done nothing to avoid his advances.

Witless fool, she chastised herself. Wasn't she the one who adamantly insisted that she was above such weakness? That she possessed a fate that did not include frivolous society or flirtations with gentlemen, no matter how absurdly charming they might be?

So why had it been only the outraged cry of a young boy that had brought her to her senses?

The disturbing question was thankfully brushed aside as Simon rose to his feet and regarded his butler with raised brows.

"Good God, Calvert, what is about?"

Holding the struggling child by the collar of his filthy shirt, Calvert frowned with deep disapproval.

"This young scamp was caught attempting to lift your silver, my lord."

"The devil, you say," Simon growled. "Is that true?"

The thin face with too-large ears and covered with dirt twisted with fear.

"I t'ain't done nothing."

The butler gave him a shake. "I caught him with the basket in his hand, my lord."

Simon took a step forward. "Do you know the penalty for theft, young lad?"

"I said I t'ain't done nothing."

"Shall I take him to the magistrate, my lord?" the butler demanded.

"No . . ."

The lad struggled even harder, tears coming to his eyes. Claire felt her heart twist with compassion. Poor child. He was obviously terrified.

"Wait," she commanded, moving toward the tiny thief and bending down beside him.

Then, as he reluctantly calmed his attempts to free himself from the relentless Calvert, she offered him a coaxing smile.

"What is your name?"

There was a pause before he gave a loud sniff. "Harry."

"Harry, there is no need to be frightened," she soothed. "We will not harm you."

Grubby fingers rose to scrub the tears from the freckled face. The effort only smeared the dirt in a pitiful fashion.

"I t'ain't no thief."

"Of course you are not."

The butler gave a choked exclamation, clearly outraged by the implication that he was lying.

"My lord," he protested.

Simon moved to tower above them, his massive frame making the lad tense in alarm.

"Claire, I think you should leave this matter to Calvert."

"No, don't let them take me to the magistrate," the youngster squawked, turning toward his only friend in panic. "They'll hang me fer sure."

Claire longed to sweep the child into her arms and assure him that everything would be fine. What should a young boy know of the hangman? Instead, she flashed Simon an annoyed glare.

"No one is going to hand you over to the magistrate. Not if you tell the truth."

"Fah," Simon muttered, only to be rewarded with another glare.

"Did you have the basket?" she softly demanded.

Harry lowered his gaze, clearly torn between the fear of the hangman's noose and Claire's persuasive urgings. At last he lifted his head.

"Aye."

"There, you see?" Calvert breathed in righteous indignation.

"But I t'ain't wanting no silver," Harry denied.

Claire smiled with gentle understanding. "You had the basket because you were hungry, did you not?"

Harry covertly glanced at the servant holding him prisoner. He was no doubt painfully aware he could be hung as easily for a scrap of food as a candelabrum.

"Aye."

"When was the last time you ate?"

"Two days ago."

Two days? Claire experienced a surge of anger. Who would allow a mere child to go without food for such a length of time?

"Calvert, would you please retrieve the basket and bring it here?" she commanded.

The butler frowned as he glanced at the silent earl. "My lord?"

Without allowing his gaze to stray from Claire's expressive countenance, he waved a hand toward the carriage. With obvious reluctance the servant loosened his hold on the boy and backed toward the carriage, clearly prepared to rush back at the first hint of trouble.

Ignoring both Calvert and Simon, Claire regarded the boy shifting his feet in a nervous fashion.

"Where do you live?"

The boy's wariness only deepened. "About."

"Have you run away?"

The eyes widened in fear. "I t'ain't going back. I'd ruther be hung."

Claire caught her breath. Rather be hung than return home? How dreadful.

"Back where?" she gently demanded, knowing she must possess all the facts if she were to help him.

A trembling lip jutted out as if he were going to refuse to answer, then Calvert returned with the basket of food and his resolve wavered. He was clearly starving.

Taking the basket, Claire lifted out a platter of pheasant. With a sudden lunge the lad grasped one of the delectable birds and began stuffing it into his mouth.

"The smithy," he retorted with his mouth full.

With deliberate stealth Calvert inched his way past the boy to stand at the side of Lord Challmond.

"Shall I fetch the sheriff?" he demanded in low tones.

"No." Rising to her feet, Claire turned to

ment."ment."ment."ment."ment.""ment."ment.""ment."ment.""ment.""ment."ment.""ment."ment.""ment."ment.""ment."ment."ment."ment."ment."ment."ment.""ment."ment."ment."ment.""ment.""ment."ment.""ment."ment.""ment."ment.""ment."ment."ment."ment."ment."ment."ment.""ment."ment."ment."ment."ment.""ment."ment."ment."ment.""ment."

Page 104 — *Debbie Raleigh*

face the butler and Lord Challmond with fierce determination. "You cannot punish a child for being hungry."

Emerald eyes carefully studied her flushed countenance with seeming fascination, then Simon gave a faint shrug.

"We have discovered where he belongs. He needs to be returned to his guardian." He paused with a lift of his auburn brows. "Unless you propose to leave him out here to fend for himself?"

"Certainly not. Nor do I intend to hand him over to the guardians who have terrified him into fleeing." Her hands landed on her hips in a familiar motion. "Surely even you can see that he has been ill treated?"

Simon studied the too-thin face and unmistakable welts from a whip on his bony arms. A grimace marred his handsome features.

"Then, what do you suggest?"

Claire considered for only a moment. "I shall take him to the orphanage. He shall be fed and schooled with no fear of being beaten."

Not surprisingly Simon frowned at her scheme. Young boys being sold into apprenticeship was an established practice. It provided a craftsman with much-needed labor and trained the lad in a profitable trade. In the eyes of the Crown the boy was the property of the blacksmith, and her interference would only create trouble for her and the boy.

"And when the smithy discovers his where-abouts?" he demanded.

As usual, Claire had given little thought beyond the immediate future. She raised her hands in an impatient movement.

"We shall decide that when the time arrives."

Their gazes locked for a moment as he probed the depths of her determination. Then, obviously sensing she would not give sway, he turned to cast his butler a resigned glance.

"Calvert, you may leave. Miss Blakewell and I will take the lad to the orphanage."

"But, my lord . . ." With an effort Calvert swallowed his protest and offered a stiff bow. "Very well."

Rigid with disapproval, the servant reached down to retrieve the blanket from the ground, then, collecting the forgotten violinist, he climbed into the carriage. A waiting groom urged the horses down the narrow path.

Claire slowly turned toward the gentleman at her side. Strangely her usual need to keep him at a prickly distance was melted by a sudden warmth.

"There is no need to trouble yourself, my lord. I am perfectly capable of walking the boy to the orphanage myself," she forced herself to say.

"I insist." That devilish grin returned. "And I do have a name, Claire. It is Simon."

Claire hesitated only a moment. "Thank you . . . Simon."

Two hours later Simon's groom pulled the carriage to a halt in front of Blakewell Manor. Simon could not help but breathe a sigh of relief.

Who the devil would have suspected that one small imp could prove to be so troublesome?

First had been the simple task of coaxing him into the carriage. Harry had maintained a firm believe that adults were not to be trusted. Any plea for him to place himself in their care was met with a fierce refusal. It was only when Claire had induced him into viewing the elegant carriage had he at last given in. It was obvious his desire to ride in such an impressive equipage had overcome his natural fear.

But even after placing the boy into the carriage, Simon's troubles were far from over. With unnerving speed Harry had climbed about the carriage, peering over the edge, bouncing upon the seats, and even attempting to climb next to the groom before Simon had firmly clamped him onto his lap. He had thought that he had heard the woman next to him stifle a giggle, but he had been far too occupied with the wiggling demon to notice.

Then, arriving at the orphanage, Simon had

been forced to physically carry the terrified Harry into the refurbished monastery. Thankfully an efficient, kind-faced lady had soon taken charge of the child and with an ease he could only envy had managed to coax the boy into following her to the kitchen. Relieved to have his burden lifted, Simon prepared to leave, only to be outmaneuvered by the devious Miss Blakewell, who insisted he view the establishment from the attics to the cellars, introducing a bevy of well-scrubbed children and a handful of staff. She had also ensured that he promised a ludicrously large donation before allowing him to return to the carriage.

Now he could only smile in rueful resignation. His carriage was marred with grubby hand-prints, his boots were scuffed, and he had no doubt that his toes were bruised. Hardly the romantic afternoon of seduction he had so carefully planned.

Still, he discovered that he did not regret his day spent with Claire. For the first time since his return he had been allowed to glimpse the tender, kindhearted girl whom he had known as a young lad.

Stepping out of the carriage, Simon turned about to assist Claire down. Amazingly she did not snatch her hand free the moment she was safely upon the courtyard and instead, glanced up with a faint smile.

"Thank you, Simon. You were very good to Harry."

He wisely chose not to reveal that the young scamp had been fortunate not to be tossed over the side of the carriage.

"It was nothing."

"And I am very sorry about your boots."

Simon heaved a rueful sigh. "Not nearly as sorry as my valet is bound to be. He takes each scuff as a personal insult."

"Perhaps he will be more understanding when he realizes the wonderful deed you were performing."

Simon gave a sudden laugh, well able to imagine the deep shock to his valet.

"He is more likely to douse me with laudanum in fear I have developed a brain fever."

She lifted her brows, although Simon did not miss the hint of amusement in the depths of her magnificent eyes.

"You do not often perform good deeds?"

"None that involve thieving orphans and innocent maidens," he informed her in dry tones.

An expression of satisfaction settled on her delicate countenance.

"Then perhaps you will not be so eager for a picnic on the next occasion."

"On the contrary. I am most eager. We were, after all, interrupted at a most inopportune moment."

With a deliberate motion he lifted her hand to his lips and kissed the slender fingers. He cursed the soft kid gloves that kept him from feeling the warmth of her skin.

Eyes wide, Claire snatched her hand from his intimate grasp.

"My lord," she protested.

"Simon," he corrected her.

"I must go."

"Wait." He blocked her retreat with his large form. "Will you ride with me tomorrow?"

"I fear that I must help Father with his accounts."

"That cannot take the entire day."

"And I arrange the flowers at the church tomorrow."

"We can go in the afternoon," he insisted.

She paused, clearly longing to refuse, then, turning to glance at the large manor house, she gave a reluctant nod of her head.

"Very well," she said in grudging tones. "That would be lovely."

Simon narrowed his gaze, a stab of suspicion piercing his heart.

Why, the shameless vixen!

She was still clearly determined to use him for her own mysterious purpose.

Well, he would teach her not to trifle with a gentleman, he acknowledged. Eventually he would discover the reasons for her strange behavior, and in the meantime he would sweep her off her feet with his irresistible charm.

A smile of anticipation curved his lips as he offered an elegant bow.

"Until tomorrow, my dear."

Climbing back into the carriage, Simon gave his groom the signal to proceed, and with a smooth jolt they were sweeping out of the courtyard and along the short path to Westwood Park. His thoughts lingered on the unpredictable Miss Blakewell and how best to set about his plot of seduction.

It would not be easy, he thought with a rueful shrug. His picnic had been meant to melt her resistance and urge her to confess her devious scheme. Unfortunately she was clearly unimpressed with the more obvious romantic ploys, while he had been all too susceptible to the lure of her innocent kisses.

He would clearly have to be very, very clever.

Still brooding on a variety of plots as they arrived at Westwood Park, Simon climbed down and ordered his groom to change horses and return to the courtyard. Then, striding into the foyer, he made his way to the library, where he crossed to the Sheridan desk and pulled out a leather sack containing several pound notes. He was on the point of leaving when the familiar form of Locky entered the room.

"Well, well, Challmond," Locky drawled.

Simon turned to meet his friend's piercing scrutiny with a mild lift of his brows.

"Yes?"

"I just heard the most astonishing tale."

"Indeed?"

Locky strolled farther into the room, a mysterious smile softening his blunt features.

"Yes. I halted at the local inn for a cup, when a chap came in and claimed that he had caught sight of Lord Challmond driving Miss Blakewell with a small lad seated upon his knee."

Simon was not surprised that the rumor was already circulating throughout the neighborhood. His position in the area had always made him a source of interest and speculation, a fact he had found decidedly unnerving when he was younger.

"That is astonishing."

Locky eyed him squarely. "But is it true?"

"As a matter of fact, it is," Simon admitted.

"Egad." Locky gave a disbelieving shake of his head. "Are you feeling quite the thing?"

"I have never felt better," Simon retorted. Then, as his companion gave a sharp burst of laughter, he narrowed his gaze. "What?"

"Quite frankly I never thought I would see the day when you would willingly spend the afternoon with a marriageable maiden, no matter how lovely. And now there is a mysterious child."

Simon's own lips twitched in response to Locky's amusement. It was true enough that he went to inordinate lengths to avoid debutantes. Matchmaking mamas had long ago given up hope of luring him to the altar. It was little wonder his current behavior seemed a bit peculiar.

"Be assured the scamp does not belong to me," he reassured with a chuckle.

"And Miss Blakewell?" Locky demanded.

Simon shrugged. "It was an innocent picnic."

Locky gave a disbelieving snort. "There is nothing innocent in a gentleman entertaining a young lady. You taught me that yourself."

"Do not fear, Locky, I am merely satisfying my curiosity."

"The battle cry of every gentleman before they tumble into the parson's mousetrap."

Simon brushed aside the absurd warning with a wave of his hand. He was in no danger of such a terrible fate. Soon enough he would grow bored with his game. Until then, he meant to enjoy himself.

"Tell me, Locky, why should a lady who has taken a violent dislike to a gentleman suddenly accept his every invitation?"

Caught off guard by the abrupt change of subject, it took Locky a moment to respond.

"Coercion?" he at last hazarded.

That had been Simon's first thought as well, but after considering Claire's fiery temperament, he realized she would be burned at the stake before being coerced into anything.

"No."

Locky lifted his hands. "A change of heart?"

Simon smiled with sardonic amusement. "Unlikely."

There was a pause before Locky gave his final pronouncement.

"Then, she wants something."

"Yes, but what?" Simon muttered.

"I haven't the faintest notion."

"Neither do I, but I intend to discover." Simon placed the money bag into his coat. "Care for a trip to the village?"

Locky gave a shake of his head. "I have already been to the inn."

"Actually I have to call on the blacksmith." Locky eyed him in surprise. "Whatever for?"

"I wish to purchase his apprentice."

"Egad."

Seven

The gray stone church tucked on the edge of the village was a simple building with a lofted ceiling and unadorned bell tower. It was nothing out of the ordinary; certainly it could not compare to the Walkhampton church or those in Exeter, but as always Claire felt a sense of peace as she entered the shadowed vestibule and crossed to the altar.

Although she always enjoyed arranging flowers for the church, today Claire was more eager than usual to seek the quiet serenity that the church offered.

Laying down her large bundle of flowers freshly picked from the greenhouse, she added water to the bronze urns and tossed aside the faded blooms.

Beginning with the greenery, Claire set about arranging a pleasing bouquet. For moments she sternly concentrated on the task at hand, then, quite against her will, the memories of the previous afternoon began teasing at the edge of her mind.

Poor little Harry, she thought with a tiny

pang. To think of the child alone and frightened in the woods for two entire days was heartrending, especially when it was combined with months of abuse from that horrid blacksmith. Of course, he was safe now, she reassured herself. The orphanage would take good care of him, and somehow she would discover a means of protecting him from the blacksmith. Even if it meant smuggling him out of Devonshire.

Perhaps she would ask Lord Challmond to help, she thought with a renegade smile.

He had certainly proven to be unexpectedly good with young Harry. What other gentleman would have endured a decidedly filthy lad climbing about his carriage and ruining his boots? Simon had even allowed him to sit upon his lap. Hardly the actions of a sophisticated rogue.

Of course, that kiss . . .

With a sharp hiss Claire abruptly put an end to that train of thought. Memories of his kisses had occupied far too much of her time. She would be better served to mind what she was doing and put aside the dangerous pleasure she had experienced in his strong arms.

Moving to the second urn, Claire was nearly finished when a shrill female voice pierced the peaceful silence.

"Claire, there you are."

Suppressing the urge to flee in horror, Claire instead forced herself to turn slowly to watch Lizzy march up the aisle with obvious determination.

"Hello, Lizzy."

"Dearest Claire," Lizzy cooed. "How are you?"

Claire longed to inform her that she had been splendid until that moment, but her ingrained manners forced a smile to her stiff lips.

"Passable."

The hard, assessing gaze swept over Claire's simple muslin gown in a cinnamon shade with a seed-pearl trim.

"What a charming gown."

"Thank you."

Lizzy's own gown was a brilliant blue silk that had clearly cost a small fortune.

"I had hoped I might find you here," Lizzy continued.

"Indeed?"

Coming to a halt, Lizzy carefully held her gown off the stone floor and peered about the dusty shadows with a sniff.

"What a ghastly relic," she complained in lofty tones. "It is only to be hoped that the new earl will see fit to sponsor renovations."

Claire instantly bristled. This church was where her parents, her grandparents, and generations of Blakewells had attended service, as well as the distinguished Challmond family. It was clearly good enough for them.

"This is a place of worship, not a front parlor to be refurbished with every passing fashion. I should hope that the earl would donate his charity to more worthy causes."

A flare of annoyance darkened Lizzy's eyes before she forced herself to flash Claire an arch smile.

"Such as your orphanage, you mean?"

"It is certainly worthy."

"It is rumored that Lord Challmond visited the orphanage only yesterday."

Claire drew in a sharp breath. For heaven's sake. A person could not slip out of their door without the entire village discussing it, she thought in exasperation.

"Yes, he did."

"Along with you and a small lad."

"Yes," Claire agreed.

Lizzy gave a coy laugh that scraped over Claire's nerves.

"He is very handsome, is he not?"

"The small lad?" Claire deliberately misunderstood. "Yes, indeed, Harry is quite splendid."

Lizzy's lips fractionally tightened. "I was referring to Lord Challmond."

Claire shrugged in a nonchalant manner. "I suppose he is not utterly revolting."

Refusing to be put off, Lizzy batted her lashes. "And quite charming. He is, you know, considered the catch of the Season in London."

Claire deliberately lifted her brows. "Lizzy,

you have not fallen victim to Lord Challmond's attractions, have you?"

"Certainly not," the woman snapped before
regaining control of her composure. "He is
obviously intrigued with you."

Claire frowned with suspicion. It was obvious
that Lizzy had deliberately tracked her to the
church and that she had deliberately shifted
the conversation to include Lord Challmond.

But why?

It took only a moment for realization to hit.
Why, the scheming . . . jade! She was obviously attempting to discover whether Lord
Challmond was going to sweep Claire off to
Westwood Park and out of Blakewell Manor. It
would certainly solve her own troubles. After
all, she could not wish to reside in a home
with a grown daughter any more than Claire
wished to obtain a mother a mere year her
senior.

She felt her features stiffen with irritation.
"I am unconcerned if he is intrigued or not."

"But surely . . ." Lizzy frowned at Claire's
casual disregard for the honor being bestowed
upon her.

"What?"

"Surely you must be pleased by his attentions?"

"Why should I be?"

"You cannot wish to remain a spinster?"

Did she?

The memory of warm lips caressing her own

sent a shiver through her body, then, with a ruthless precision, Claire thrust the traitorous thought aside.

Being a spinster was precisely what she wished.

"I am quite satisfied with my life," she retorted with more force than necessary.

Lizzy regarded her with rising irritation. "And what will you do should your father choose to remarry?"

At last they came to the reason Lizzy had sought her out.

"That is hardly likely." Claire waved an indifferent hand. "But even if he should, that would not affect me."

"You could not remain at Blakewell Manor."

"Why not?" Claire demanded.

"It could hardly be comfortable there for you with a new mistress in the house."

Claire narrowed her gaze. "Not comfortable for me or the new mistress?"

"I am thinking only of you, dear Claire," the woman spat out.

"How kind of you, dear Lizzy," Claire retorted. "But there is not the slightest need."

Their gazes clashed, then Lizzy conjured a cold, decidedly cunning smile.

"Do you not have an aunt who resides in Bath?" she at last inquired. "Perhaps she would allow you to reside with her."

Claire unconsciously curled her hands into

tiny fists at the woman's audacity. How dare she!

"I have no intention of residing in Bath, now or ever."

"Certainly that is for your father to decide?" Lizzy retorted, then, belatedly noting the dangerous heat simmering in Claire's eyes, she wisely chose to retreat. "Now you must excuse me. I have promised your father I would give him my opinion on new drapes for the library."

Nearly trembling with anger, Claire whirled back to the flowers and angrily began stuffing them into the urn.

The woman was beyond the pale, she seethed. She had all but threatened to have her removed from her own home, either by marrying her off to Lord Challmond or having her exiled to Bath.

And then, to actually imply Henry Blakewell would request her opinion on refurbishing Blakewell Manor . . . fah.

Shoving the last of the flowers into the urn, Claire whirled about, only to discover Ann Stewart watching her with raised brows.

"Oh . . . Ann."

The older woman smiled as she stepped forward.

"Good morning, Claire." She deliberately glanced toward the maltreated flowers in the urn. "Is something troubling you?"

"Lizzy Hayden is troubling me," Claire promptly replied.

"Mrs. Mayer? What has she done?"

"She has set her cap firmly in my father's direction."

"Ah." A faint smile curved Ann's mouth.

"Even worse, my father has informed me that he has grown weary of waiting for me to present him with an heir and has decided to take matters into his own hands."

Not surprisingly it took Ann a long while to comprehend her meaning. Then she gave a startled blink.

"You mean that he is actually considering Mrs. Mayer as a wife?"

Claire shuddered. "Yes."

"Oh, my."

"It is insufferable," Claire burst out. "I would as soon reside in the stables as with that cunning harpy."

Ann's brows drew together in vague bewilderment. "I cannot conceive your father would choose Mrs. Mayer. Even though I dislike speaking ill of others, there is not a soul in the neighborhood who is not aware of her shallow nature and spiteful tongue. And she has certainly made no secret of the fact she will wed only for money."

"My father has clearly taken leave of his senses."

"Perhaps."

Sensing Ann's distraction Claire reined in her simmering emotions.

"What is it?"

"It is just so odd," Ann murmured, then added after a shake of her head. "In any event, I did not come here to speak of Lizzy Hayden."

"Thank God," Claire muttered.

"I wish to discuss Lord Challmond."

Claire rolled her eyes. What happened to the days when she never heard the names of Mrs. Mayer or Lord Challmond? They seemed too far in the past.

"Not you too?"

"Excuse me?"

The delicate features hardened. "Lizzy has already attempted to marry me off to the earl."

Ann's soft laugh echoed through the silent church. "I am not quite so daring. But I must say that I was quite surprised by his generosity."

Feeling suddenly foolish, Claire blushed. Of course Ann was referring to Lord Challmond's hefty donation. She had been a fool to leap to the conclusion that she had meant anything else.

"Yes. The orphanage will be fortunate to have him as a patron," she swiftly agreed. "Indeed, I was thinking we might use a portion of his contribution to build the greenhouse I have always desired. The children could help us to grow their own vegetables all year long."

"Yes, we must check on the cost of such a project," Ann agreed, absently moving to straighten the lopsided flowers. "But I was not referring to Lord Challmond's contribution to the orphanage, as generous as it was."

"Oh?"

"I was referring to the fact he had offered the blacksmith a considerable sum to release his claim on little Harry."

"What?" Claire breathed, her mind reeling. Lord Challmond had paid the blacksmith to release Harry? Why?

Ann turned back to regard her in surprise. "You did not know?"

Claire gave a slow shake of her head. "No."

"Mrs. Laury overheard Lord Challmond call on the blacksmith yesterday afternoon. She claimed Lord Challmond offered a ridiculous sum to free Harry from his apprenticeship."

He must have gone straight from her to the village, Claire acknowledged. But why had he not revealed what he intended to do?

"I cannot believe it."

"She also said that the earl threatened to have the blacksmith sent to the gallows if he were to abuse another boy," Ann continued with a hint of relish.

"Goodness."

"She claimed that the blacksmith was on his

knees, begging for forgiveness, before the earl left."

A sudden surge of gratitude overrode her wary disbelief. She might not comprehend why Lord Challmond should go to such trouble for a stray waif, but she was fiercely glad that he had. Only a man of his power and position could intimidate the bully of a blacksmith into releasing his claim on Harry.

"I only wish I could have seen the horrid man on his knees," she retorted with a slow smile. "He deserved to be horsewhipped."

Ann smiled with gentle understanding at her less than charitable delight.

"Yes, it was certainly a disgrace, the manner he treated Harry," she agreed, then she regarded Claire in a knowing manner. "Still, what could possibly have convinced Lord Challmond to go to such an effort for one small boy?"

A thoroughly ridiculous hint of color bloomed in Claire's pale cheeks.

"I haven't the least notion."

"No?"

"No," she denied in firm tones.

Ann shrugged as her lips twitched with inner amusement.

"Well, he has certainly proven himself to be a true gentleman. We shall be forever in his debt."

Keeping her expression deliberately bland, Claire gave a faint nod.

"Yes."

Ann regarded her for another moment, then, with a small laugh, she moved forward to lightly pat Claire's arm.

"I shall see you at the orphanage tomorrow."

"Of course. Good day."

Claire deliberately waited until Ann had moved out of the church and across the yard to the large vicarage. She wanted to be alone to ponder Lord Challmond's odd behavior.

At last Claire gathered her now-empty basket and made her way to the side door and out into the late morning sunlight. She barely noted the gentle warmth of the rare spring sunshine or the faint scent of wildflowers coming into bloom. Instead, she considered the inordinate amount of trouble Lord Challmond had gone to for one small boy.

A half hour later Claire walked into the courtyard of Blakewell Manor no closer to comprehending the truth, only to discover the gentleman occupying her thoughts was just arriving in his glossy open carriage. Her heart gave a pleasurable flip as he vaulted onto the cobblestones attired in a smoke-gray jacket and pale silver breeches. It was utterly unfair, she thought as he crossed toward her, that one gentleman should possess such an overabundance of devilish charm.

"Good afternoon, Claire." He offered her an elegant bow.

Her gaze unknowingly searched his handsome countenance with piercing intensity.

"My lord."

"Simon," he instantly chided.

"Simon."

He frowned, appearing to easily sense her distraction. "Has something occurred?"

She paused, then gave a restless motion of her hand. "Do you mind if we walk instead of riding today?"

He lifted an auburn brow in mild surprise. "Not at all."

Turning, he motioned toward the waiting groom. "Keaton, you may return to Westwood. I will walk back."

"Very well."

With an experienced flick of his whip the uniformed groom sent the matched grays out of the courtyard. Returning his attention to Claire, Simon reached out to firmly place her hand onto his arm and slowly led her toward the scythed parkland. Waiting until they were away from the manor, he glanced down at her tiny countenance.

"I am sorely afraid to inquire what has you so somber."

"I have just discovered what you have done for Harry."

"Ah."

She came to a halt so that she could view his dark features.

"It was very kind of you."

His mouth twisted with wry amusement. "Does it surprise you that I can be kind?"

"No," she denied, refusing to be distracted. "I just cannot comprehend why you should go to such trouble."

"Do you not?" Without warning he lifted a hand to gently stroke her cheek. "It is because I wished to please you."

The ground seemed to lurch beneath her feet as Claire gazed into the beautiful emerald eyes. Her thoughts blurred at the soft caress of his slender fingers, and for once her sharp tongue was unable to utter more than a breathy whisper.

"Oh." She blinked and tried once again. "Oh."

Eight

Simon was quite certain he had never seen a more enchanting sight than the tangled emotions rippling across Claire's expressive countenance. Suddenly the ugly encounter with the ill-tempered blacksmith and the large amount of pounds he had paid over to the brute were all worthwhile. Even the knowledge that he was at the center of the village gossip paled into insignificance. All that was important was the beautiful creature standing before him.

His fingers moved to tilt up her chin for a closer inspection.

"Are you blushing, Claire?" he lightly teased.

With a tangible effort she struggled to retrieve her cool composure.

"Certainly not." She stepped back from his lingering grasp. "I presume you must be teasing me."

Regretting the loss of contact with her satin skin, Simon gave a shake of his head.

"Not at all."

She frowned in disbelief. "Why should you wish to please me?"

If she had been one of the London beauties who had hunted him for years, Simon would have presumed she was angling to trap him into an admission of admiration. Now he simply chuckled at her obvious innocence.

"Why does any gentleman wish to please a young lady?"

Her frown became a positive scowl. "Lord Challmond, you shall catch cold trying that nonsense with me."

"Oh?" Simon tilted his head to one side, unable to resist temptation. After all, she had instigated the game herself. "I must admit, I am rather baffled."

"Why?" she demanded warily.

"I presumed that your agreement to bear me company was an indication that you were encouraging my interest." He deliberately paused as she drew in a sharp breath. "Am I mistaken?"

"I . . ."

"Yes?"

The blue eyes flashed with annoyance at his teasing. "You could not possibly be interested in me."

"Why not?" he demanded, his gaze sweeping over her stiff frame. "You are the most extraordinarily beautiful woman I have ever encountered."

With a sharp motion she turned away, clearly unnerved by his persistent flirtation.

"We were discussing Harry."

"Were we?"

"Yes." She paused to collect her composure. "I wish you to know that it was a wonderful thing that you did. Indeed, I do not even know how to thank you. I never expected you to go to such an effort for poor Harry."

It was Simon's turn to be uncomfortable. Although pleasing Claire had been only one of the reasons he had confronted the blacksmith, he had no desire to be seen as a saint. He was far too conscious of the fact that he had been a sad disappointment as the Earl of Challmond to the village and his neighbors.

"I did very little, Claire," he protested in quiet tones.

She turned about to shake her head. "That is not true. It is because of you that Harry will be safe."

He shrugged. "I have no more wish to see a child abused than you, my dear."

"It is only to be hoped that the dreadful man will not harm any more children."

Simon briefly recalled the terrified blacksmith begging for mercy. Like most cowards, he bullied only those weaker than himself. When faced with Simon and Locky, he had swiftly lost his nerve. And to ensure he remained suitably cowed, Simon had promised he would personally place the noose around the man's fat neck if he mistreated another lad. The cunning scoundrel had, however, managed to extract a small fortune to give up his claim on Harry. Money that was meaningless to Simon except for the annoyance of lining the pockets of a common blackguard.

"I sense he will hesitate to repeat such behavior," he assured his companion.

Her eyes abruptly softened. "I shall ensure that Harry realizes just what a fortunate young man he is."

A sharp flare of distaste stabbed through Simon's heart, and he gave a firm shake of his head.

"No."

She blinked at his abrupt tone. "Excuse me?"

"I do not wish Harry to know anything beyond the fact that he need no longer fear the smithy."

Not surprisingly she regarded him in confusion. "But why?"

He hesitated. A private man, he rarely revealed his inner emotions. Only with Philip and Barth did he ever speak openly. But he had no desire to see the stray imp saddled with the same troubles he had endured.

"Because I did not free him from the yoke of abuse only to burden him with the yoke of obligation," he at last admitted.

"I do not understand."

Of course she did not, he thought with a

sigh. She had always been the one to help others. How could she possibly realize it was not a simple matter to accept such help?

"Charity can be a dangerous business, my dear." His lips twisted with long-suppressed emotions. "Especially if you are the one receiving the charity."

"You are speaking of the old earl?" she demanded.

A twinge of guilt shot through Simon.

"I do not mean to imply that he was not a decent man or that he in any way mistreated me," he insisted, not wishing to speak ill of the man who had given him so much. "But he did ensure that I was never allowed to forget just how obligated I was to his generosity in not producing a male heir to claim the title, not to mention the sacrifice in paying for my education and allowing me to reside at Westwood Park. And, of course, there was always the reminder that it was only his goodwill that kept my mother receiving his monthly allowance. If I disagreed with him or did not measure up to his expectations, I was sternly reminded that both I and my family owed him a debt that could never be repaid."

Momentarily forgetting she desired to keep him at a firm distance, Claire unconsciously reached out to lightly touch his arm.

"That is horrid."

He covered her hand with his own, savoring the scent of lilacs that filled the air.

"He did not mean to be horrid. In his mind he had done me a great service in taking me out of the vicarage and bringing me to Devonshire to be trained as the next Earl of Challmond. It was my duty to appreciate it."

She studied him for a moment. "And that is why you avoid Westwood Park?"

Simon was taken off guard by her soft accusation. Few of his most intimate acquaintances questioned his lack of interest in his estate. They simply presumed that he preferred London and the delights of the metropolis. Only Philip and Barth had suspected there was more to his disregard than he admitted, but they had known better than to pry. Now he felt oddly exposed beneath the steady blue gaze.

"Perhaps."

"Do you wish the earl had not brought you to Westwood Park?"

"At times," he admitted. "Although I knew that I would one day be earl, I missed my family, especially my mother. It is not easy to be separated from everything you have known."

"Do you see them now?"

"No." He grimaced. "I visited shortly after I left school, but it was hardly a success."

She unwittingly stepped closer, unaware of just how distracting the warmth of her slender body was to a susceptible male.

"Why not?"

"My brothers found my presence discomforting and my mother obviously felt guilty at having allowed me to be taken by Lord Challmond, even if it was for my own good." An unconscious pain flared through his eyes. The visit had been more than just awkward. From the moment he had arrived at the vicarage he had been out of place with his Weston-cut coats and stories of his pranks with viscounts, earls, and even a duke. And always had been the hint of loss deep in his mother's eyes that had tugged at his heart. "They were quite relieved when it was time for me to leave."

Her fingers tightened on his arm. "So you have no one?"

A gentleman could spend a lifetime gazing into those lovely blue eyes, he decided as his blood began to stir.

"I have Locky. And, of course, Philip and Barth."

"Who?"

Simon smiled, wondering how the two were faring. Philip was no doubt breaking hearts throughout London, while Barth was settling in Kent and preparing to marry his biddable Miss Lawford.

Did they ever recall the strange old Gypsy and her absurd claim they would all find true love? he wondered. Then as swiftly as the thought appeared, he shoved it aside.

What the devil had made him recall the ridiculous hoax?

"They are gentlemen who have become as

close as any brothers," he explained, determinedly lighting his tone. "They saved my life during the war."

Her lips parted in what might have been dismay. "You were injured?"

He shrugged. "A trifling wound."

"I did not know."

The urge to play upon her obvious sympathy was quickly smothered. There were far too many young soldiers in genuine need of sympathy. Instead, a sudden glint entered his eye.

"Would you care to see the scar?"

She immediately pulled away, her expression chiding. "Simon."

He gave a chuckle. "Will you join me tomorrow for a picnic?"

"I do not think that would be proper," she informed him in pert tones.

"If you like, I shall bring Locky as a chaperon."

She firmly placed her hands on her hips. "And promptly send him off to fish?"

He merely laughed again at her accurate assumption. "If you will recall, our last picnic was interrupted," he drawled. "The least you can do is grant me another."

As always, she appeared impervious to his attempts at charm.

"Surely you have better means of passing the day?"

He held her gaze. "None at all."

A hint of confusion rippled over her features. "I . . ."

"Claire."

The sound of Henry Blakewell's call had them both turning toward the manor, where the older gentleman hurried in their direction. Simon suppressed a stab of annoyance at the interruption. He longed to carry Claire off to some remote location, where they would not be constantly pestered by others. Of course, he belatedly acknowledged, the arrival of Mr. Blakewell might prove to be an unexpected blessing. It had not passed his notice that Claire was far more likely to accept his invitations in the presence of others. One of the many pieces of her puzzling behavior. He even managed a smile as the gentleman halted beside them.

"There you are, Claire."

The pale features settled into an unreadable expression.

"Father."

Mr. Blakewell turned to Simon. "My lord, what a delightful surprise."

"Mr. Blakewell."

"I hope you will stay to lunch?"

"Unfortunately I am promised to join Aunt Jane." Simon sensed Claire's relief.

"A pity." Mr. Blakewell frowned, then instantly brightened. "Perhaps later in the week?"

"I should be delighted." He sent a wicked

glance in Claire's direction. "For now, however, I am futilely attempting to convince Miss Blakewell to join me for a picnic tomorrow."

Mr. Blakewell glanced at his daughter in pleasure. "What a lovely notion, do you not think, Claire?"

The tiny nose flared as if she found the notion anything but lovely. Still she was careful to keep her stiff smile intact.

"Of course, but tomorrow is the day I help at the orphanage."

"Nonsense." Mr. Blakewell waved a negligent hand. "You devote far too much time to that orphanage. It is high time that you enjoy yourself a bit."

Claire's mouth opened as if to argue, then, noting her father's gathering frown, she reluctantly turned toward Simon.

"Very well," she conceded, narrowing her gaze as she continued. "But I must at least help with the morning lessons. I shall meet you in the far meadow."

Simon had a distinct sense that there was something brewing behind that mask of innocence, but with her father standing so close, he could only bow in agreement.

"Until tomorrow."

"Yes, tomorrow."

Simon eyed her for a suspicious moment, then, with a nod toward Mr. Blakewell, he turned to cut through the parkland. He angled toward the small pathway that would lead to Westwood Park, his thoughts dwelling on the lovely and mysterious Claire. Quite unexpectedly he discovered himself whistling as he walked. It had been years since he whistled, he acknowledged with a vague sense of surprise. Surely his rare goodwill was not due to Miss Blakewell? After all, he was seeking out her company only to punish her for daring to trifle with his emotions. And, of course, to discover the reasons for her odd behavior.

But strangely, whenever she was near he promptly managed to forget everything but the delight of making her eyes sparkle and the temptation of her soft mouth.

Perhaps he did have a fever of the brain, he thought with wry amusement. It was a preferable explanation to the thought he simply found Claire irresistible.

Still whistling, he crossed the low bridge and went up the sloping hill to the main house. Brain fever or not, he intended to make tomorrow a day Claire would never forget.

"Dashed rum business if you ask me," Locky complained as he surveyed the large blanket covered with platter upon platter of delicacies. His glare lingered on the rose petals scattered over the ground and the bowl of chocolate delicately carved in the shapes of cats.

Simon smiled as he opened a bottle of champagne. "Yes, so you have said."

Locky crossed his arms across his barrel chest. "Bad enough to eat lunch off the ground as if we were back fighting Boney," he groused. "Now I discover that I am to play nursemaid to a pair of lovebirds."

"Hardly lovebirds," Simon denied, more out of habit than dislike at being romantically paired with Miss Blakewell. "And as for being a nursemaid, I prefer that you make yourself scarce." He waved a hand toward the distant river. "No doubt there are any number of trout waiting to be caught."

Locky's expression hardened with suspicion. "What are you plotting?"

Simon assumed an air of wounded innocence. "Why, nothing more sinister than a lovely afternoon with a beautiful woman."

"You have not forgotten she is an innocent maiden?" Locky demanded.

"I have not forgotten." Simon regarded his friend with a hint of impatience. "I have no intention of seducing her with you just a few feet away."

Locky deliberately glanced over the elegant luncheon, then toward Simon's claret coat and buff breeches that would not have been out of place in the finest drawing room.

"Then, what are your intentions toward Miss Blakewell?"

His intentions? Simon resisted the urge to inform Mr. Lockmeade that his intentions were none of his concern. He had never interfered in Locky's private affairs, especially not when it concerned a young lady.

Then, with an effort, he eased his momentary irritation. His friend was simply ensuring that he had not taken complete leave of his senses.

"My only intention is to enjoy a picnic with Miss Blakewell," he assured in firm tones.

A small, rather mysterious smile sudden lightened Locky's blunt features.

"I wonder."

Simon lifted his brows. "What?"

"I am curious whom you are attempting to fool," Locky murmured. "Yourself or me."

"Ridiculous," Simon snorted. Really, Locky was behaving as if the simple meal were an extraordinary event. Then a distant sound brought a glint of anticipation to his eyes. "Ah . . . I hear a carriage approaching."

Simon gracefully rose to his feet, his fingers holding a single red rose. It took several moments before a broken nag came into view, followed by an ancient cart filled to near overflowing with noisy children. Seated on the driver's bench was a dark-haired, handsome woman with a serene smile, and holding the reins was the familiar blue-eyed minx who had begun to haunt his thoughts with alarming frequency.

"Ha." Locky regarded the approaching horde with a wide smile.

Simon gave a slow shake of his head. "Good God."

"It appears, Challmond, that once again you have been outgunned."

For a moment Simon glared at the approaching cart, feeling a distinct sense of annoyance that his afternoon alone with Claire had been stolen away. Then, without warning, he gave a sudden laugh.

"Vixen."

Nine

The sound of children's laughter echoed through the air, combined with an occasional splash as Locky and Miss Stewart unsuccessfully attempted to teach the youngsters the finer points of fishing without actually joining the fish in the narrow stream.

It was a delightful scene, even for a gentleman who had been spoiled by the most elegant entertainments throughout England and Europe. And Simon oddly discovered that he was not nearly so disappointed as he would have suspected to share his meal with the chattering scamps.

How could he be?

Although it was far from romantic, there was a certain satisfaction in the open delight that had crossed the children's faces at the lavish feast. And surprisingly he had discovered himself settling one of the tiny imps upon his lap and helping him consume the delicacies.

It had been a meal filled with overturned plates, sticky fingers, and a great deal of laughter.

Not that he would admit his enjoyment to Miss Blakewell, he acknowledged as he turned to glance at the maiden seated on the blanket next to him. She deserved a bit of punishment for so neatly tripping him into his own trap.

Stretching out his long legs, he leaned upon one elbow and studied her pure profile.

"I suppose that you are pleased with yourself?"

Her expression was prim although her full lips twitched with amusement.

"I do not know what you are referring to, my lord."

"You know quite well I did not intend to share our picnic with a pack of noisy scamps."

"No?" Her tone was unmistakably smug. "I thought you would be pleased to see for yourself how well Harry is doing."

Simon allowed his gaze to turn toward the slender boy darting through the other children with evident pleasure. A sense of satisfaction warmed his heart.

"He does seem remarkably changed."

"And so smart," Claire informed him. "He shall soon catch up with the rest of the children in his studies."

Simon returned his attention to the woman at his side. "Is he in need of anything?"

"He is content for now," Claire assured him, then, after a pause, she turned to offer him a suspiciously innocent smile. "Of course, all of the children enjoy outings such as this. We could certainly use a new cart for the orphanage. The one we possess has decidedly seen better days."

He gave a sudden bark of laughter. The devious wench. What other woman of his acquaintance would so easily ignore the honor of his attentions and instead cleverly use his interest to further her charitable endeavors?

None, of course.

The women of his acquaintance were far more interested in landing a titled husband than in concerning themselves with those less fortunate.

"And, of course, with a new cart you would certainly need a new horse to pull it about," he teased in light tones.

Claire waved a hand toward the battered cart and swaybacked nag.

"Yes, I fear old Athena will soon be unable to pull herself up the lane, let alone twenty children and a cart."

"You are shameless, Miss Blakewell," he informed her with an amused glint in his eye. "I am only relieved that you have turned your talents to charitable deeds. You would no doubt be able to fleece the most cunning of cardsharps with that innocent smile and cunning intelligence."

"You did ask," she pointed out with little apology.

"So I did." His gaze stroked over her face.

"And I shall be happy to purchase a new cart and horse."

Her smile made his breath catch. "Thank you, Simon."

"Any more requests?"

She gave a surprised laugh at his charitable mood. "Several, but I shall not try your generosity further today."

Simon silently acknowledged she was a fool. At the moment he might be willing to promise the throne of England to see that smile again. Instead, he shifted closer, breathing in the scent of lilacs.

"How very obliging of you."

"I can be obliging when I choose," she retorted in pert tones.

His gaze deliberately moved to the tempting softness of her lips.

"What a very provocative notion, my dear."

She drew in a soft breath before hurriedly turning her attention to the giggling children.

"Mr. Lockmeade appears to be enjoying himself." Her voice was even, but there was a hint of color in her cheeks.

Simon smiled as he reluctantly allowed her to turn the conversation. He was well enough acquainted with the stubborn chit not to press his luck.

"Yes. I would never have suspected he would be so patient with children."

Claire watched as Locky helped one of the younger children hold on to his pole. At his side Ann Stewart laughed at something he said.

"He will make an excellent father."

Simon gave a slow shake of his head. "I doubt that he will ever wed."

Claire was clearly caught off guard. "Whyever not?"

"He has never felt comfortable among society," Simon explained, not sure that this woman would comprehend Locky's discomfort. Claire was a woman who judged others on their inner worth. A rare quality among society. "And there are few mothers who would encourage his suit unless they were on the hunt for a fortune."

A frown tugged at her dark brows. "Any mama with sense would be delighted to welcome Mr. Lockmeade into their family."

"I fully agree."

"Indeed, he is quite above most gentlemen of supposed quality."

Simon lifted a hand in mock defeat. "You do not have to convince me, Claire. As far as I am concerned, Locky is one of the finest gentlemen I have ever encountered."

There was a slight pause before she turned to face him.

"And what of you, Simon?" she inquired in a deliberately light tone. "Do you intend to please some hopeful mama and choose a Lady Challmond?"

Intrigued by her uncharacteristic interest in

his private life, Simon gave a faint shrug, a devilish humor tugging on his lips.

"Duty demands that I eventually wed and produce an heir."

Something seemed to flash deep in her eyes, but her expression remained unconcerned.

"How terribly dull," she quipped. "I pity your wife."

Simon arched an auburn brow. "She shall want for nothing."

"Except love."

"I did not think you believed in love," he charged, closely surveying her delicate features.

"Of course I do," she surprised him by insisting. "I simply have no desire to experience it for myself."

His full lips twitched again. "Surely love is not something you can rationally decide whether you wish to experience it or not?" he teased. "Was it not Shakespeare who claimed that love was a 'madness most discreet'? It presumably strikes without warning and leaves a poor soul helpless beneath its power."

She gave a faint grimace. "You shall soon rival Byron if you do not have a care."

"I have no fear of that, my dear," Simon chuckled.

Pretending a supreme indifference, Claire plucked a rose petal from her cream-and-jade striped gown.

"So you view love as an unstoppable force and yet you intend to marry for duty?"

"Duty is just as an unstoppable force." Simon peered deep into her wide eyes. "Of course, a gentleman might wish for the two to be one and the same."

He had merely intended to provoke a rise from the volatile maiden. She was such a delight to tease, and he thoroughly enjoyed seeing her blush at his flirtatious remarks.

Now, however, he discovered himself lost in the blue-velvet softness. Never before had he wished to gaze into a woman's eyes. Nor had he felt as if the world were slipping away as a flutter of desire stirred his loins.

Good God, perhaps he was becoming as doddy as Byron, he thought with an odd flop of his heart.

The sound of approaching footsteps at last brought him to his dubious senses. Abruptly glancing about, he discovered Ann Stewart regarding him with an unreadable expression. For no reason whatsoever he discovered himself battling the ludicrous urge to blush.

"I must thank you, Lord Challmond." Ann smiled with her placid composure. "This is a wonderful outing for the children."

Simon gracefully rose to his feet, determinedly thrusting aside his strange reactions.

"All the credit must go to Claire, I fear," he insisted with a slight bow.

"I also wish to thank you for your very generous donations to the orphanage."

"It is my pleasure to be of assistance. I hope you will feel free to come to me if there is anything else you require."

"A most dangerous offer, my lord," she warned with a twinkle in her eye.

"I also have a request, Miss Stewart."

"Yes?"

"I wish to hire a new steward. I would be grateful if you would offer any suggestions."

"I should be happy to, my lord," Ann promised in pleased tones, then as a splash followed by several angry shouts broke the peace of the afternoon she heaved a small sigh. "Ah, I believe that it is time to return the children to the orphanage. Please excuse me, my lord."

Watching as Ann moved back toward the children, Simon was unaware that Claire had also risen to her feet. Only when she began to step away did he realize she was intent on leaving with the others.

"Wait, Claire."

She reluctantly turned back to face him. "I must help Ann."

Simon moved forward to firmly grasp her hand. "You have outwitted me today, my dear, but the battle is far from over." He raised her gloved fingers to his lips. "We shall take the field again."

For a timeless moment she allowed her hand to linger, then, with a sharp shake of her head, she pulled her fingers free and swept away. Simon remained standing on the blanket with an unconscious frown on his brow.

He was beginning to suspect that Miss Blakewell was occupying far more of his attention than was reasonable. Surely he should instead be rambling about the countryside with Locky or even enjoying the numerous invitations lying on the foyer table?

Then, glancing at her lovely face as she stooped to lift one of the smaller children into her arms, his brief unease abruptly vanished.

Why shouldn't he enjoy her companionship? She was by far the most enchanting creature in all of Devonshire. It would be far stranger if he did not seek out her company.

Suitably reassured, a small smile lightened his countenance.

He had far more important matters to ponder than why he wished to be with Claire.

Beginning with how the devil he was supposed to purchase a new cart and horse.

"Blimey."

Glancing up from the leather-bound book of poetry she had been reading aloud to the students, Claire discovered Harry standing at the back of the schoolroom with his pug nose pressed to the windowpane. She suppressed a smile. Although Harry possessed a swift intelligence, he found the structured environment of the classroom difficult to accept.

"Harry, please return to your seat," she stated in firm tones.

The boy turned to flash her an engaging grin. "It be your gentleman."

A sudden, not wholly unpleasant tingle raced down Claire's spine.

"Pardon me?"

The grin widened. "That lord you always be with."

A twittering of muffled giggles had Claire abruptly rising to her feet. It had to be Lord Challmond. What other gentleman could Harry mean? But why would he be at the orphanage?

"Children, please return to your studies," she ordered. "I shall be only a moment."

With crisp steps Claire left the schoolroom and moved down the short hall to the front entrance. Then, sternly quelling the unruly beat of her heart, she composed her features and stepped into the late morning sunlight.

Determined to present a cool composure, Claire was immediately thrown off guard as she caught sight of Lord Challmond standing beside a large horse and cart.

Although he had promised yesterday to purchase the equipage, she had never expected him to manage it so swiftly. In fact, she had presumed he would hand the task over to one of his servants and forget all about it. Now she found herself blinking in amazement.

Clearly pleased at her undeniable surprise, Simon performed an elegant bow. As always, he appeared ridiculously handsome in a deep green coat and buff pantaloons. His auburn hair shimmered with a hint of sunlight, and that heartwrenching smile tugged at his full lips.

"Good morning, Claire."

With an effort she gathered her composure. "Good morning, Simon."

He waved a hand toward the cart. "I hope you approve?"

"How could I not approve?" she demanded. "But I must admit that I am surprised."

He tilted his head in a familiar manner. "You did request a cart and horse, did you not?"

"Yes, but . . ."

"But?"

She gave a small shrug. "But I did not expect you to manage so swiftly."

He merely smiled at her blunt retort. "Does it meet your requirements?"

"It is perfect." Moving forward, Claire ignored the tingle of awareness that sent a rash of goose bumps over her skin. After a long, restless night she had reluctantly concluded that there was no reasonable explanation for her odd reaction to Lord Challmond. Instead, she concentrated on the glossy chestnut mare. "What a lovely girl. What is her name?"

Simon moved to lightly stroke the mare's silky mane. "Lady."

"Lady?" Claire repeated in unconsciously disappointed tones.

The emerald eyes shimmered with amusement. "Perhaps the children would like to choose her a new name."

"Yes." She paused, then forced herself to meet his gaze. "This is most kind of you, Simon."

Turning from the horse, he was close enough for her to feel the heat of his form through her pale apricot gown.

"Does it please you?" he asked softly.

She felt the tingles hurry through her body. "Very much."

He smiled deep into her eyes. "Good. I also have a gift for you."

"I could not accept a gift."

"You do not even know what it is," he reminded her gently.

Really, did the gentleman have to be so utterly charming? she wondered with a stab of exasperation.

"It would not be proper."

He reached out to lightly brush a raven curl from her forehead.

"And you are quite a stickler for propriety, eh, Claire?" he teased.

Her chin tilted. "Certainly."

Simon clicked his tongue at her patent lie, but thankfully he turned away from her heated cheeks to lean into the nearby cart. She frowned in suspicion as he reached beneath the seat and retrieved a black ball of fur.

"This gift will in no way offend propriety, I assure you, Claire."

He held out the fuzzy ball, and suddenly two blue eyes popped open to reveal the object was a tiny cat. Claire felt her heart instantly melt.

"Oh."

She reached out to take the enchanting creature, holding it to her chest in an instinctively protective fashion.

"She reminded me of you," Simon said softly, a rather odd expression on his handsome countenance as he studied the kitten pressed to her heart. "Raven hair with blue-velvet eyes. An angel with claws."

"She is beautiful." Claire rubbed her chin against the silky head. "Where did you get her?"

"Mrs. Foley. She was the tiniest and fiercest of the litter." He paused. "So you will keep her?"

"Of course." She did not bother to hide her pleasure. "Thank you, Simon."

"You are welcome, Claire." He stepped forward, his gaze easily holding her own. Something shimmering in the emerald eyes sent a flare of heat racing through Claire's body. His hand reached out to grasp her chin. She could have pulled away, but she found herself unable to move as his head began to lower. "Very welcome, indeed," he whispered before his mouth was claiming her own in a warm, searching kiss.

Claire quivered as the now-familiar excitement pooled in the pit of her stomach. In the back of her mind a voice cautioned that she should pull away. That only a wanton of the worst sort enjoyed the advances of a known rake. But the pleasure shimmering through her body was far too potent to battle. She gave a soft moan as his lips became more possessive, savoring the softness of her mouth. It was only the faint sound of giggles that at last pulled them apart. Raising his head with obvious reluctance, Simon closely scrutinized her dazed countenance.

"It appears we have an audience."

With a surge of embarrassment Claire glanced toward the schoolroom, where a dozen tiny faces were pressed against the window. Good God, she chastised herself, she was hardly a fit chaperon for young children. Why, she was no better than a common tart. Turning back to the amused gentleman, she stabbed him with a flustered glare.

"My lord, you really must halt your habit of kissing me."

He tilted back his head to laugh at her prim command. "But why?"

"Because it is not proper."

"Perhaps it is not proper, but it is certainly delightful," he murmured.

All too delightful, she acknowledged with a flare of panic. Suddenly she needed to be away from this disturbing gentleman. How could she possibly be expected to think in a rational manner when her heart was racing and her stomach fluttering with the most distracting sensations?

In time she would laugh at the absurd incident, she futilely assured herself. But for now she could only flee.

"I . . . I must go."

Clutching the kitten to her unruly heart, Claire turned on her heel and raced back toward the orphanage. Behind her she could hear the soft sound of Simon's laughter taunting her blatant cowardice, but for once she did not care.

She wanted only to be away from the gentleman causing such disruption in her calm life.

Ten

It was several hours later before Claire left the safety of the orphanage. It had been a struggle to concentrate on helping the students with their studies, especially when confronted with their muffled giggles. She felt a fool, and it did not help to realize that a dozen children had witnessed her folly.

At least the kitten proved a welcome distraction. The children had taken great delight in retrieving a saucer of milk from the kitchen, and each took turns holding the small animal. They had even helped her to name the kitten Portia after the character in *The Merchant of Venice*.

After helping to serve the modest lunch, Claire had at last said her good-byes, but on the point of leaving she discovered herself hesitating. She rather rudely walked away from Simon, she acknowledged with a pang. She should at least ensure that Lady was comfortably settled. Whatever her muddled feelings toward Lord Challmond, it was a most generous gift, a gift that would be of great service to the children for years to come.

Veering toward the rather dilapidated stables, Claire entered the shadowed interior. It took only a moment to discover the chestnut mare in a clean stall. The horse gave a toss of her proud head as Claire approached and gently set the kitten on a pile of hay.

"There you are, my beauty," she said in soft tones, stroking the velvet nose of Lady. "Such a pretty girl."

Lady heaved a pleased sigh as Claire continued her firm strokes, talking in low tones. She paid little heed to the passage of time until the door to the stables was pushed open and the sound of Ann's soft gasp echoed through the hay scented air.

"Goodness."

"Ann." Claire turned to regard her friend, feeling oddly uneasy beneath the piercing gaze. "I did not expect you out here."

Ann moved slowly forward, a hint of a smile curving her lips.

"When I arrived at the school, the children were filled with stories of a fancy gentleman and his gift."

Claire kept her expression deliberately unreadable. "Yes, I am certain they must be quite excited by such a fine cart."

Ann gave a slow nod of her head. "It is a most wondrous gift. We shall be forever in Lord Challmond's debt."

"He has been most kind."

"Kind, indeed," Ann agreed before allowing her suppressed laughter to fill the air.

Claire's unease increased as she cast Ann a narrowed gaze.

"What?"

"I fear the children were less excited by the cart than the kiss they observed you giving Lord Challmond."

Drat the aggravating gentleman, she seethed in embarrassment. She was an intelligent woman with a clear sense of her own purpose, and yet he managed to make her appear as ridiculous as a susceptible schoolgirl.

"I did not kiss Lord Challmond," she absurdly denied. "He kissed me. And much against my will, I might add."

Ann gave a mock blink of surprise. "Do you mean to say that he forced his attentions upon you?"

Claire longed to bury herself beneath a pile of hay; instead, she could do no more than square her shoulders and hope she did not appear as foolish as she felt.

"Not precisely," she amended.

"Then, you wished him to kiss you?"

"No . . . I . . ."

Ann smiled gently at her flustered bumbling.

"Forgive me, Claire. I did not mean to tease," she said, moving forward. "I am very happy that Lord Challmond has taken an interest in you. The orphanage has certainly

benefited from his attraction. And you have
never appeared happier."

Claire felt the blood fade from her face. For
goodness' sake, what was Ann thinking? Lord
Challmond interested in her? Absurd. He was
a gentleman who could have his pick of beauties, whether they be ladies or those of easy
virtue. The mere notion that he was interested
in more than whiling away a few dull hours
with her was simply ridiculous.

"That is absurd," she at last stammered.

Ann regarded her with mild surprise. "What
is absurd?"

"Lord Challmond is not interested in me."

"Of course he is," Ann insisted, seemingly
baffled by Claire's obtuse refusal to see the
truth. "Why else would he go to such lengths
to be in your company?"

"He merely enjoys taunting me."

Ann's eyes widened as she gave a tinkling
laugh. "Not even you are that naive, Claire."

For no reason Claire felt her color return
with a fury. The memory of warm lips stroking
and teasing her own sent a quiver of delicious
heat through her body.

She was a wanton maiden, she told herself
sternly.

"You are greatly mistaken, Ann," she forced
herself to mutter.

"Perhaps." Ann shrugged in disbelief. Then
the pathetic cry of the forgotten kitten had
the older woman's attention shifting to the

black ball of fur upon the hay. "Where did this adorable kitten come from?"

Chastising herself for neglecting her newest pet, Claire reached down to pluck the disgruntled Portia from the hay. Placing it against her heart, she reluctantly met Ann's curious gaze.

"Mrs. Foley," she hedged.

"Mrs. Foley?" Ann demanded in surprise.

"Yes."

"Mrs. Foley sent the orphanage a kitten? How very odd."

Drat, she sighed. She should have simply headed for home when she had the opportunity.

"Actually Portia is for me," she reluctantly confessed.

"Ah." A sudden flash of understanding rippled over Ann's countenance. "I do not suppose that Lord Challmond was responsible for bringing you the kitten?"

Claire heaved a weary sigh. Lord Challmond had a great deal to answer for, she thought in exasperation. Even when he was not near he created troubles in her life.

"I fear that you shall have to save your inquisition until a later date," she muttered in defensive tones. "I promised Father I would be home for lunch."

"Of course." Ann battled to hide her amusement. "I shall see you tomorrow."

Feeling ridiculously self-conscious, Claire walked past her friend and into the afternoon sunshine. She did not pause on this occasion, but instead hurried across the yard toward a narrow path. Although she could easily have a carriage at her disposal, Claire preferred to walk when the weather permitted, although today she would not have been averse to the convenience of a coach. The sooner she was in the privacy of her home, the sooner she could regain command of her composure.

Why had she ever thought to use such a disturbing gentleman to fool her father? she wondered as she stepped over a fallen log and headed into the thickening woods. Her father had yet to rid himself of Lizzy while her own well-ordered world was in turmoil. Perhaps it would be best to abandon her rather desperate scheme before she discovered herself in dangerous waters.

After all, there were other gentlemen in the neighborhood who did not make her heart leap and her knees unnaturally weak.

Dwelling on her confused thoughts, Claire crossed a narrow bridge that marked Westwood Park. It was far shorter to cut through the pasture than to skirt the vast estate. She had little concern of encountering the bothersome earl at such a remote location.

Surprisingly, however, she had taken less than a dozen steps when a large shadow crossed the path. She came to an abrupt halt, half expecting her thoughts to have conjured Lord Challmond. But the thick frame and ruddy countenance had nothing in common with the handsome Simon, and her leaping heart abruptly plunged to her toes. Although she had no desire to run across Lord Chall-mond, it would certainly be preferable to Mr. Foster.

She unconsciously grimaced as his beady eyes made a slow inspection of her stiff form.

"Well, well. If it ain't Miss Blakewell," he drawled in ugly tones.

Claire tilted her chin as she held the sleeping Portia close to her.

"Mr. Foster."

"Quite the meddlesome female, ain't you?" he accused.

"Excuse me?"

Foster stepped closer, filling the air with the stench of stale whiskey and an unwashed body.

"Always sticking that bloody nose where it don't belong."

An unfamiliar flare of fear stabbed though her heart. Although she had faced Foster on more than one occasion, it had never been so far from others. And, of course, there had always been the knowledge the greedy scoundrel would never risk his comfortable position by attacking a wealthy young maiden.

Now he had nothing to lose, and Claire could sense a drunken disregard in his swaggering stance.

Still, she had no intention of revealing her

unease. Not to an out-and-out bounder.
"Please stand aside."

He ignored her lofty command as his eyes
narrowed. "You got me thrown out."

"You were thrown out because you stole
money intended for Lord Challmond's tenants," she corrected him in cold tones.

"Bah," he spat out. "What does a nob like
Lord Challmond care of farmers?"

Once Claire would have agreed with his dis-
paraging comment; now she gave a sharp tilt
of her chin.

"He happens to care a great deal."

Foster spit on the ground, nearly hitting
Claire's skirt. "He cared for nothing until you
interfered."

Claire took a pointed step backward, her expression one of cold disapproval.

"I merely pointed out that the cottages were
falling into disrepair. It was hardly a secret,"
she said. "And if you had been performing
your duties in a competent manner, you would
not have been asked to leave."

"What do you know of how I worked?"

She ignored the little voice that warned her
to walk away from the scoundrel.

"I know that you spend your days at the inn
and your nights gambling away money intended for the estate."

His face became even redder. "Easy for a
lady such as yerself to sneer at the likes of
me."

"I do not sneer at you, Mr. Foster," she denied.

An evil expression hardened his features. "Well, mayhap I think you do," he growled as he stepped even closer. "Mayhap I think you owe me something for the trouble you've caused."

Another stab of fear pierced her heart as she acknowledged just how alone she was with the angry man.

"Stand aside, Mr. Foster, or I shall scream."

"And who would hear?" he mocked, clearly as aware of their isolation as she. Then the glittering gaze dropped to Claire's heaving breast and her heart nearly stopped with fright. Good Lord, what disaster had she tumbled into now? she wondered with a surge of panic. Why, oh, why hadn't she brought the carriage like any sensible maiden? Or at least brought along a proper chaperon?

She swallowed heavily, wondering how she was going to save herself when she realized the villain's gaze was firmly attached to the necklace she had forgotten she wore.

"Now, be a luv and hand over them fine pearls. They might ease the pain of being turned off with no place to go."

Ridiculously Claire discovered her fear being replaced with a burst of anger. The necklace had belonged to her mother, and while it was certainly not the most valuable piece of jewelry, it was her most sentimental. She wasn't about to hand it over to a common bully.

"Never," she exclaimed in fierce tones.

Foster bared his teeth as his grimy hand rose toward her neck.

"If you won't hand them over, then I'll take them."

"No."

Knowing he was far too large to fight off, Claire did the only thing she could. Gathering her skirts in one hand, she clutched the sleeping kitten with the other and with a burst of speed dashed into the thick trees.

Behind her, Claire could hear Foster give a loud curse, then the crashing sounds of his pursuit through the underbrush.

Although Claire did not often have the opportunity to dash about the countryside, she was wise enough to keep her head low and to dart through the thick bushes rather than struggle against them. Her slender frame helped her to slip into even the narrowest gaps, and soon the sound of Foster's labored breathing began to grow fainter and fainter.

Claire gave a silent prayer of thanks for the large amount of whiskey Foster had no doubt consumed as she angled toward Westwood's great house. She was quite certain that Foster could have easily overcome her if he weren't half foxed.

On the point of believing she might actually escape unscathed, Claire risked a glance over her shoulder. It proved to be a costly mistake as her foot caught on an exposed root and she abruptly lunged forward. Turned to an awkward angle, Claire was helpless to halt her tumble forward and with a faint cry she heavily hit the ground.

Her last memory was the sight of a large stone and the certain knowledge it was directly in line with her forehead. Then a sharp pain exploded in her head and everything went perfectly black.

Seated in the leather wing chair beside the black marble chimneypiece, Locky watched as his companion paced the length of the library for the hundredth time. On the low table was a tray overflowing with sandwiches and cakes, and a pot of tea that had been forgotten, as well as the decanter of brandy Simon had ordered, only to leave it neglected as he continued his restless pacing.

Locky hid a small smile. He had never witnessed his friend so discomposed. Not that he entirely blamed Simon. He had been distinctly rattled when he had stumbled across Miss Blakewell lying upon the ground with blood trickling down her forehead. But by the time he had carried her up to the house he managed to convince himself that she merely knocked herself unconscious after tripping over a root in the pathway.

His arrival at the house, however, caused a near riot. One glance at the battered beauty in his arms, and Simon exploded into action. He plucked the maiden from Locky's arms, demanding the surgeon to be called, that tea be fetched, that water be boiled, and the yellow room opened as he swept up the stairs. Then he planted himself on the bed next to Miss Blakewell, refusing to budge until the surgeon at last threw up his hands and cried that he could not examine his patient with his lordship hovering over her like a mother chick with its egg.

Banished from the sickroom, Simon had begun his ceaseless pacing, on occasion marching into the hall and glaring up the long flight of steps. Returning from yet another circuit, Simon roared in frustration. "What the devil is taking that surgeon so long?"

Locky stretched out his legs and crossed them at the ankles.

"It has been less than half an hour."

Simon frowned in displeasure. "I should send to London for a doctor."

"She has a bump to the head, Challmond, not a mortal wound."

Simon reined his temper with an effort. The devil take it, how could he meekly stand aside and wait? He had never been so frightened as when Locky had entered carrying Claire in his arms. Just for a moment a pain that he had never felt before clutched at his heart and he nearly fell to his knees in response. The only means he had of keeping the panic at bay was to keep himself busy, even if it was only walking from one end of the room to the other.

"We both know that head wounds can be dangerous."

"It is a bump, not a wound," Locky pointed out with exaggerated patience. "No doubt we both have received worse falling off our mounts when we were bosky."

Simon regarded his friend with open displeasure. "You appear remarkably unconcerned."

"You wrong me, Challmond," Locky argued. "When I came upon Miss Blakewell lying upon the ground, my heart nearly halted. All I could think was to get her to Westwood Park as swiftly as possible. But since you are clearly determined to be anxious enough for all of England, I have resigned myself to the role of keeping you from any foolish actions, such as riding off to London for a doctor, when there is a perfectly capable surgeon upstairs."

Simon grimaced in a rueful manner. "I hate this waiting," he admitted by way of apology, then determinedly turned his thoughts to the other worry nagging at the edge of his mind. "What could have happened to her?"

"Difficult to say." Locky gave a faint shrug. "Perhaps she was startled by a small animal."

Simon swiftly dismissed the suggestion. "You

do not know Miss Blakewell if you think she could be frightened by a mere animal."

"Surely all ladies are terrified of mice and rats?"

Simon gave a decisive shake of his head. "Not Miss Blakewell."

"Then perhaps she simply tripped. I did notice a root sticking out of the path."

It was a perfectly reasonable explanation, but Simon remained unconvinced. Why would Claire be on a path leading directly to Westwood Park? After their delicious interlude that morning, he would have bet good blunt she would go out of her way to avoid his presence. And how had she managed to overlook a large root and tumble hard enough to knock herself unconscious?

"Perhaps," he murmured in disbelieving tones. "Whatever the reason, she should not have been alone in those woods. I have warned her more than once." His stern words were cut short as a small, nearly baldheaded gentleman entered the room. Moving forward, Simon regarded the surgeon with impatience. "Well?"

Remarkably calm despite the large earl looming over him, Mr. Cassel slipped on his greatcoat.

"Miss Blakewell appears to be coming about."

"Thank God." Simon felt his entire body quiver with relief. "What of her head?"

"She had taken quite a blow."

Simon paled. "Then, it is serious?"

"I do not believe so, but any injury to the head should be treated with great caution."

Simon shot his companion a sour glance. "My thoughts precisely."

"I wish her to remain abed for the next two days," the surgeon commanded. "I shall return then to ensure she is well enough to get up."

"Of course," Simon promised, only briefly considering Miss Blakewell's reaction to her predicament. He did not care if he had to tie the stubborn chit to the bedpost to make her remain.

"If her condition worsens, send for me immediately."

Simon stepped forward as Mr. Cassel prepared to leave. "May I see her?"

"Only for a few moments," the elderly man warned. "She is not to be overly exerted."

Simon gave a conceding nod, then glanced toward his friend.

"Locky, would you see to our guest? I wish to discover if Miss Blakewell is in need of anything."

Locky immediately rose to his feet. "Of course."

"Thank you." Simon offered both gentlemen a distracted bow, eager to be with Claire. "Have the bill sent to my secretary."

Mr. Cassel bowed with rigid formality. "Your servant, my lord."

Simon swept past the surgeon and into the hall. On the point of climbing the steps he was halted by the sight of his housekeeper.

"Ah, Mrs. King." He waited for the older woman to join him by the stairs. "Miss Blakewell will be staying with us for the next few days."

"The poor dear," Mrs. King breathed, no doubt having heard the gossip running rampant through the mansion. "Is she badly wounded?"

"The surgeon does not believe so, but we do not wish to risk removing her to Blakewell Manor."

"Certainly not."

"Could you please request Aunt Jane to remove to Westwood Park?" he commanded. "I believe it would be best to have a chaperon if only for appearance's sake."

"Yes, my lord."

"And send a message to Blakewell Manor to inform Mr. Blakewell what has occurred."

"Anything else, my lord?"

Simon gave it a moment of thought.

"You might also inquire if Miss Blakewell has any favorites that Cook can make for her," he at last decided. "We want her stay to be as comfortable as possible."

Unable to suppress his need to assure himself that Claire would indeed survive, Simon turned and vaulted up the stairs.

Standing below, Mrs. King watched the earl's hurried retreat with a growing smile. She had a distinct sensation that Miss Blakewell's visit would prove to be anything but comfortable.

Eleven

Simon entered the large bedchamber with blatant disregard for propriety. What did he care if it was proper or not to be alone with a young maiden in such an intimate setting? He had waited what seemed to be an eternity to be at her side.

Crossing the polished wood floor, he felt his breath catch at the sight of Claire lying upon the vast bed. How fragile she appeared with her raven hair spilling across the crisp white pillows and her tiny countenance marred by an ugly bruise on her temple. An intense, almost frightening surge of pain clutched at his heart.

He wished to pull her into his arms and protect her from the world, to ensure that she was never harmed again.

He gave a rueful shake of his head at the direction of his thoughts.

Gads, but this chit had managed to make a mare's nest of his usual composure, he acknowledged with a pang of unease.

A faint sound from the bed had him sternly

thrusting aside his absurd fancies as he moved to perch on the feather mattress. As he reached out to softly stroke the satin curls from her forehead, the thickly lashed lids fluttered upward.

Dazed blue eyes drifted over his dark countenance, clearly baffled by the sight of him so close.

"What . . . where am I?" she breathed.

His fingers absently lingered against the warm silk of her skin.

"Westwood Park."

She frowned in confusion. "How did I get here?"

"In a moment." He studied the bump on her temple. "How do you feel?"

"Awful," she croaked.

"I fear you appear even worse."

"Thank you." She gave a rueful grimace, only to wince in pain.

"Would you like a drink?"

"Yes. Please."

Simon reached to the side table, where a decanter of well-diluted wine had been left. He poured a half glass, then with exquisite care he slid an arm beneath Claire's shoulders and lifted her to a more upright position. He placed the glass to her lips.

"Here we are." He helped her take several sips before setting the glass back on the tray.

Sinking back into the pillows, Claire slowly

lifted a hand to press against the growing bruise.

"Oh."

Simon flashed her a dry glance. "I am no doctor, but I would suggest that you not press on that amazing lump."

Her hand dropped as she gave a slow shake of her head.

"What occurred?"

He regarded her for a long while. "You do not recall?"

"No."

"Locky discovered you in the west woods," he explained. "You were lying upon the ground with that very nasty lump on your head."

Her brows drew together in bewilderment. "How odd."

"Do you know why you were in the woods?" he demanded, hoping to jog her memory.

She paused as she attempted to piece together her rattled thoughts.

"I remember being at the orphanage and then beginning to walk home," she said slowly, then she gave a startled gasp.

"What?"

"It was Mr. Foster," she breathed.

"Foster?" Simon stiffened with fury. Damn that worthless cad. If he had so much as touched Claire, he would have him strung from the nearest tree.

Claire shuddered. "Yes."

"That bloody . . . I should have run him from the estate days ago." He cursed his own stupidity. "What did he do?"

The blue eyes darkened. "He just suddenly appeared and blocked the path ahead of me. He blames me for having lost his position."

Simon struggled through the reluctance to cause her further distress and the need to discover what precisely had occurred.

"Did he . . . touch you?"

It took a moment for her to realize the import of his words. Then a sudden color tinted her pale skin.

"No, he wanted my pearls." A familiar, unrelenting expression hardened her features. "But I would not let him have them."

Simon's burning anger was in no way eased by her proud boast. Good God, was this female touched in the head? Did she even realize the danger she had placed herself in?

"You fool," he growled in exasperation. "You should have given them to him. What are pearls when your own life is in danger?"

Not surprisingly her chin jutted upward at his chiding. He had already learned that she would rather have her tongue removed than admit she might have been in the wrong.

"These pearls belonged to my mother." Her hand lifted to the delicate necklace hung about her throat. "I am certainly not handing them over to that villain."

"Why am I not surprised?" he gritted out,

then, with an effort, he swallowed his words of reprimand. For now he wished to concentrate on his unsavory steward. "Did he strike you?"

Her fingers returned to press lightly against the lump. "I do not believe so. I began running from Mr. Foster, but before I could reach the edge of the woods I tripped over something in the path." She paused before giving a vague shrug. "I remember nothing after that."

Simon briefly considered her explanation. The fact that Claire was alive and her pearls still intact revealed something had managed to sway Foster's evil intent. He would not willingly have walked away from the maiden he blamed for his downfall or the necklace that would seem like a fortune to a man in his position.

Once again he cursed himself for not considering the danger in allowing him to remain in Devonshire. With a bit of money and a few favors called in, he could no doubt have had the scoundrel deported.

Which was precisely what he intended to happen when Foster was caught, he told himself fiercely. That was, if he didn't hang him first.

"Foster must have been frightened that he had managed to kill you, or perhaps he heard Locky approaching," he muttered.

Her fingers slowly dropped. "Is it very bad?"

He drew in a deep breath and attempted to

ease the tension clutching at his muscles. Soon he would discover Foster and make him pay dearly for daring to harm this woman.

Very soon.

"I have been assured that you will live." He deliberately lightened his tone.

"I apologize if I have given you any trouble."

He could not prevent a sudden laugh. "When are you not giving me trouble, my little cat?"

"Please do not call me that." Her lashes fluttered in charming confusion before abruptly widening in dismay. "Cat. Oh. Portia."

He tilted his head to one side. "Pardon me?"

"My kitten," she cried. "I must have dropped her when I fell. Do you have her?"

Simon gave a rueful shake of his head. The kitten had been the last thing on his mind when she had been carried in. Indeed, he had forgotten all about his impetuous gift. Now he was certain he would be reprimanded for his perfectly reasonable oversight.

"No, I am afraid that Locky found only you."

With thorough disregard for her weakened condition, Claire struggled to lift herself off the bed.

"I must go and retrieve her."

Simon hastily grasped her shoulders to firmly press her back into the pillows.

"Do not be absurd, Claire, you cannot leave this bed."

"But I must," she fretted. "Poor Portia is far too young to survive on her own."

"I will send a battalion of servants to scour the woods with a stern command they are not to return without dear Portia."

She eyed him in suspicion. "Do you promise?"

"Yes, I promise."

She reluctantly relaxed back into the pillows, but Simon oddly found his hands lingering.

"I hope she is not injured."

"I am certain that she is in better condition than yourself," he said in dry tones.

"How can you be so indifferent?" She favored him with a chiding frown. "She is so tiny."

Simon found himself decidedly vexed at her charge of indifference. It was not his fault that she had been tramping through the isolated woods without so much as a maid.

"At least she possesses more sense than her mistress."

Her mouth thinned with displeasure. "I beg your pardon?"

"What the devil were you doing in those woods by yourself?"

"I was walking home."

"And you are so destitute that you cannot afford a carriage or even a maid to walk with you?"

She shrugged off his clinging hands with obvious pique.

"It is only a short distance."

"Clearly it is far enough to be of danger to a young maiden on her own," he pointed out with indisputable logic.

Predictably Claire refused to admit her fault and instead regarded him with a mutinous expression.

"If you had never hired such a man as Mr. Foster, I would not have been in danger."

The sheer injustice of her accusation nearly stole his breath. For God's sake, was it not bad enough that she had nearly frightened him to death without attempting to place him at fault?

"You cannot possibly blame me for your own bloody-minded stupidity."

"You did hire the man."

Simon rolled his eyes heavenward. "Why can you not just admit that you were wrong to be tramping about the countryside on your own?"

The blue eyes flashed. "I certainly will not."

"You are a fool."

He could almost hear her teeth clench in fury, and he felt a certain satisfaction in having pricked her composure.

"I hardly think that is any of your concern."

"You made it my concern when you nearly got yourself killed on my land."

"Well, I will not trespass on your hospitality for long."

Once again she attempted to struggle upright, and once again he firmly pressed her back onto the pillows.

"Actually you will be trespassing on my hospitality for at least the next two days."

He felt her stiffen in wary disbelief. "What?"

"The surgeon has insisted that you not be moved for at least two days."

"But that is impossible," she breathed with an unflattering hint of horror in her tone. "I cannot remain here."

Simon smiled with mocking amusement. If he had ever considered himself as irresistible to the fairer sex, this vixen had certainly disabused him of such a ludicrous notion.

"You most certainly can and will," he retorted.

"But . . ."

"Yes?"

She worried her full bottom lip before lifting her hands in a restless motion.

"I would feel much more comfortable at Blakewell Manor."

"Perhaps, but the surgeon has commanded that you remain here, and that is precisely what you will do."

For a moment their gazes locked in a silent battle as Claire struggled to control her willful temper.

"You, sir, are a bully," she at last muttered, her expression reminiscent of a sulky child's.

"And you are a stubborn wench," he retorted, then, with a shake of his head, he heaved a rueful sigh. Blast the aggravating chit. She made him behave as if he were no more than twelve. "Ah, Claire, I believe that you could annoy a man to his grave."

She gave a faint snort. "You are a fine one to talk."

"Let us agree that we are both ill natured, overly proud creatures with a habit of expecting others to bend to our will," he conceded. "Let us also agree that we are more or less stuck with each other for the next two days."

"I am not ill natured."

He chuckled at her petulant tone. What would this woman think if he were to tell her that on a dozen different occasions he had had cunning females attempting to be thrown from their horses or twisting their ankles outside his home to gain access to his presence?

She would no doubt inform him they were batty.

"Can we attempt a cease-fire for the duration of your stay?"

Her thick lashes dropped to hide her eyes. "It appears that I have little choice."

"Do not fear, Claire, you shall soon be mended and well away from my annoying presence," he drawled, then slowly rose to his feet.

"Now, I suppose I should begin to organize the rescue mission for Portia."

Her lids abruptly rose, and Simon felt an odd twinge in the center of his chest at the hint of vulnerability in the blue-velvet depths.

"My lord . . ."

"Simon," he softly corrected her.

"Simon," she conceded as she plucked at the sheet covering her slender frame. "I am sorry."

He stilled at her startling words. "Sorry?"

"I do not mean to appear ungrateful," she forced herself to say. "It is just that I dislike imposing upon you."

Barely aware he was moving, Simon leaned down to brush her cheek gently.

"There is no imposition between friends, Claire." His gaze probed deep into her wide eyes. "And for all of our enjoyable skirmishes, I do hope that we are friends."

There was a pause before she slowly gave a nod of her head.

"Yes."

With a decided effort Simon resisted the urge to taste the sweet temptation of her lips. For the moment she was wounded and in need of his mercy. Only the most dastardly cad would take advantage of her momentary weakness.

Soon she would be back in fighting form with her claws intact, and he would satisfy the burning need to hold her in his arms.

"Rest easy, my dear," he murmured. "I will ensure that nothing troubles you while you are in my care."

Twelve

Turning back from the window, where a blackbird perched to enjoy the afternoon sunlight, Claire studied the chessboard laid upon the mattress. For a moment she puzzled over the various pieces before slowly lifting her gaze with a sense of amused exasperation.

"You cheated," she accused Simon, regarding the darkly handsome countenance with pretended outrage.

The magnificent emerald eyes widened with mock innocence. "What?"

"You told me to look at the blackbird in the window and then you moved my rook."

"Ridiculous." Grasping the chessboard, Simon moved it onto a side table. Then he settled himself more comfortably in the chair pulled next to the bed. "Gentlemen do not cheat. Especially not to best a mere maiden."

Claire ignored the deliberately provocative words. In the past day and a half she and Simon had developed a remarkably peaceful companionship. Beginning with dinner the evening before, he had set a mood of easy informality. And, of course, his favor had risen immeasurably when he had produced the tiny black kitten that had merely yawned at Claire's shriek of delight.

That morning he had arrived with a tray of breakfast and Aunt Jane, who had promptly disappeared into a far corner with her needle-work. They enjoyed a surprisingly spirited discussion on the turmoil in Europe and sweeping troubles of the Corn Laws. He had then set about teaching her to play cards, only to be thoroughly trounced, followed by twenty questions, then chess. He had clearly been unaware that her father had taught her such parlor games since she was old enough to talk. Now she regarded him with a decidedly smug expression.

"You knew that I was about to checkmate you, and so you cheated."

"Infamous." His gaze swept over her raven hair that was loosely braided and the white lawn dressing gown that modestly covered her thin frame. There was a darkening to the emerald eyes that she could not know was in appreciation to her Madonna-like beauty as she leaned back into the great pile of pillows. "I will not stand aside while my honor is besmirched."

"Ha. What honor?" she demanded.

"Ah." His hands dramatically lifted to press to his wide chest. "A direct hit."

She couldn't help but laugh at his absurd

antics. Really, it was little wonder the gentleman was branded a rake. He possessed far more charm than any gentleman had a right to.

"You, sir, are a cad of the highest order."

"No, merely a badly humiliated gentleman who has been thoroughly beaten at every match I have attempted against you," he corrected her. "A wiser soul would no doubt retreat from the field in shame, but I, mademoiselle, am made of sterner stuff. I shall eventually discover your weakness."

"And what if I have no weakness?" she demanded.

He slowly leaned forward and firmly grasped her slender fingers.

"Then I shall simply enjoy the search."

That pleasurable warmth fluttered in the center of her stomach.

"Ridiculous."

"So what is it to be?" he demanded in low tones. "Fencing, boxing, a race about the—"

His teasing words came to an abrupt halt as a shadow fell across the open doorway. With an unconscious frown at the interruption Claire turned in time to watch the intruder sweep into the bedchamber. The odd feeling of contentment was swiftly destroyed as she recognized the curvaceous form of Lizzy Hayden.

As always, the widow was richly attired in a bishop's-blue satin gown that was daringly cut.

Her hair, far too pale for nature, was arranged in stiff curls to frame her rouged countenance.

Entering the chamber, she made a swift inspection of the elegant furnishings, lingering on the cast-silver pier table and mirror and French bronze mantel clock. Her calculating gaze made an equally assessing survey of Lord Challmond, obviously appreciating the broad shoulders beneath the molded coat and aquiline features. For no reason whatsoever Claire found her dislike of the woman suddenly sharpened.

Unaware that her fingers were tightly gripping Simon's, she smoothed her countenance to a cool mask of composure as Lizzy at last turned to offer her a patently false smile of pity.

"My poor, poor Claire."

"Lizzy."

"I was simply aghast when I learned what had occurred. Simply aghast," she proclaimed in melodramatic tones. "So of course I rushed over to dearest Henry's to see how you go along."

Of course, Claire acknowledged with cynical humor. The woman would use any excuse, no matter how obvious, to rush to dearest Henry.

"How kind."

"He assured me that you were recovering, but I insisted that I see for myself."

"There was no need."

"There was every need," Lizzy insisted in a cloying tone. "We are, after all, like family."

Claire recoiled as if she had been slapped. Egad, what a horrid notion!

"Hardly family," she protested in cold tones.

Undaunted, Lizzy gave a toss of her head. "Oh, la, Claire, of course we are. Indeed, I have promised Henry that I shall do whatever necessary to ease your discomfort."

Claire clutched at Simon's fingers in dismay. The only means this woman could have of easing her discomfort was to leave and never return.

"Thank you, Lizzy, but Lord Challmond has adequately eased any discomfort I might possess."

"Oh?" A coy expression settled on the narrow countenance as Lizzy deliberately regarded their clasped hands. "How very kind of you, my lord."

Simon gave a vague shrug, his gaze narrowed in a speculative manner.

"Not kind at all. It has been my pleasure."

"Yes, I can imagine." Lizzy gave an arch laugh that set Claire's teeth on edge. "What gentleman would not wish to have such a lovely maiden beneath his roof?"

Simon slowly turned to regard Claire's growingly heated features with an arched bow.

"What gentleman indeed?"

"And one that is so talented," Lizzy continued.

The brow arched higher. "Oh?"

"Yes, she has managed her father's household for years."

Simon's gaze never wavered from Claire's embarrassed features.

"Remarkable."

"And such a deft hand with the servants. They simply adore her."

Simon's lips twitched. "Who would not?"

"And, of course, you are quite aware of her wonderful deeds with the needy."

"Of course."

Claire could endure no more. For goodness' sake, she felt like a horse on market day.

"Thank you, Lizzy, but you failed to mention my needlework is ghastly, that I detest playing the pianoforte, and see little use in dabbing paint on a canvas. I also have no patience with the usual society entertainments."

Lizzy's shrill giggle echoed through the room, competing with the soft snores of Aunt Jane in the corner.

"Really, Claire, what will Lord Challmond think?"

"That I am quite lacking in female graces," she muttered, wishing she could crawl beneath the bedcovers and disappear. "It is hardly a secret throughout the neighborhood."

A hint of chagrin rippled over Lizzy's countenance before she was forcing a stiff smile.

"You must not mind her peculiar sense of humor, my lord."

"I do not mind at all," Simon drawled, his thumb running a soft path over Claire's knuckles. "Indeed, I find it as enchanting as all her other qualities."

"There, you see, Claire," Lizzy cried in delight.

Claire could see all too clearly. Lizzy was so desperate to rid herself of an unwelcome stepdaughter that she could not realize just how absurd it was to imagine a gentleman of Simon's standing would consider Claire as a potential bride.

Claire, however, was under no such illusion. Simon was clearly a gentleman who instinctively flirted with every maiden that crossed his path. The fact she had claimed indifference to his charms would only pique his interest.

And, of course, that was precisely what she preferred, she told herself sternly.

The past hours in Simon's company had been undeniably pleasurable, but she had no place in her ordered life for charming rogues.

"When you become better acquainted with Lord Challmond, Lizzy, you will discover his own sense of humor is quite peculiar," she retorted in dry tones.

There was another grating giggle. "Silly, silly Claire. Well, I must hurry along. I have one of Cook's delicious sponge cakes for Henry." A smug smile curled the thin lips. "Someone must care for the darling gentleman while you are gone, Claire."

A strangled noise was caught in Claire's throat as Lizzy offered Lord Challmond a small dip before sweeping from the room. Someone care for her father, she seethed. He was a grown man with a house full of servants, not a helpless child.

And since when did her father even like sponge cake?

"Sponge cake for dear Henry?" Simon murmured. "Almost like family?"

With an effort Claire thrust aside her dark thought and turned toward her companion.

"Pardon me?"

The emerald eyes twinkled with wicked humor. "Do I detect a lady on the hunt to become the next Mrs. Blakewell?"

Claire shuddered even knowing that he was merely attempting to tease her.

"Do not say such a ghastly thing," she pleaded.

The dark head tilted to one side. "You do not wish for your father to wed again?"

"Certainly not to Lizzy Hayden."

"I agree she is a trifle . . ." He struggled to conjure a delicate term for the harridan. "Forward."

"Forward?" Claire gave a loud snort. "She is a managing, conniving jade who has no interest in my father beyond his position in society and his fortune."

"Hardly an unusual reason for a sensible female to choose her husband."

Her eyes flashed with annoyance. She would like to see how calm he would be if Lizzy were angling to become a part of his family.

"She has also all but threatened to have me banished to Bath if she lures my father to the altar."

Simon gave a startled shout of laughter. "Good God. I give her full marks for courage. Not many would dare to cross the dauntless Miss Blakewell."

She regarded him narrowly. "This is not amusing."

With an effort he struggled to suppress the laughter still smoldering in his eyes.

"So what of your father?" he at last demanded. "Has his head been turned by the charms of Mrs. Mayer?"

"Of course not," she denied, giving little thought to her impetuous words, or where they were leading. "Not even Father is that much of a fool. All he desires is . . ."

"What?" he prompted as her words trailed to a halt.

"Nothing."

"You cannot halt now, Claire," he commanded in stern tones. "What does your father desire?"

Cursing her own stupidity, she met his gaze squarely. "An heir."

He blinked as if caught off guard by her blunt retort.

"You mean he wishes for a male issue?"

"No. Any heir besides the one he already possesses."

He gave a shake of his head. "But why?"

"Because." She struggled to dampen the revealing blush. It was simply so embarrassing to discuss such an intimate subject with this gentleman. "Because he realizes that I have no interest in providing him with grandchildren."

"Ah." A slow realization dawned as he gave a soft chuckle. "Poor Claire. You are clearly caught between Mrs. Mayer as a stepmother and lowering your noble fate to produce a Blakewell heir. How distressing for you."

She didn't know what the devil he found so amusing.

"I have no intention of either having Lizzy in my home or producing heirs."

"No?"

"No," she said in firm tones.

He regarded her for an unnerving moment. "I sense 'something rotten,' as Shakespeare would say," he murmured. "What are you plotting, my dear?"

Claire suddenly realized that she was in danger of revealing more than her father's absurd decision.

"Nothing."

The emerald gaze narrowed as Simon studied her guarded expression. He was obviously pondering her unwitting revelations. Then his hand tightened on her fingers.

"Why, you devious vixen."

With an effort Claire attempted to keep her countenance unreadable.

"What?"

"That is why you forced yourself to endure my company and accepted my invitations," he accused her.

She gave a small shrug. "I do not know what you mean."

"You were using me to try to persuade your father that he had no need to wed Mrs. Mayer."

"You, sir, possess a most vivid imagination."

He gave a slow shake of his head, a hint of something that might have been annoyance glinting in his eyes.

"Not vivid enough, or I would have suspected the truth from the beginning." His full lips twisted with a decidedly sardonic smile. "And you label Mrs. Mayer as a managing, conniving female."

Claire's mock innocence crumbled beneath his unjust accusation. How dare he cast her in the same ilk as Lizzy Hayden? She did not intend to lure him into marriage for mere money. Or pretend to care for those closest to him with every intention of having them exiled to Bath.

"I did not connive," she denied with a tilt of her chin. "You were the one to thrust your attentions upon me. I merely . . . used them to my advantage."

Simon was glaringly unimpressed with her

defense. An odd tension hardened the handsome features.

"Very convenient."

Claire felt a swift and surprising stab of guilt. She had in some regard behaved in a less than truthful manner. And she had manipulated his presence to deceive her father. Perhaps she had connived a bit.

Absurd, she firmly chided the renegade thoughts. He was the one to seek out her company. If he had not persistently pestered her with his attentions, she would never have come up with the far-fetched notion in the first place.

"As a matter of fact, it was not convenient at all," she retorted in haughty tones.

"No?"

"No."

He regarded her defensive expression for a moment, then slowly his annoyance faded. His hand loosened its grip on her fingers to stroke softly up her arm. A dangerous smile curved his lips at her instinctive shudder.

"So, my little cat, what punishment do you deserve for toying with my affections in such an infamous manner?"

"I did nothing of the sort," Claire denied, briefly wondering if every woman reacted with such exquisite delight to his merest touch. Was this what made a rake so irresistible? This magic to set a lady's blood aflame? All she knew for certain was that his soft caresses were making it decidedly difficult to concentrate on the matters at hand. "Indeed, I went to painful lengths to assure you that I possessed no interest in your supposed affections."

With a smooth motion he shifted from the chair to the side of the bed, his hip intimately pressed to her own.

"A ploy that only deepened my regard," he murmured in a husky tone. "What gentleman could resist the desire to capture such an elusive heart?"

Placing his hands on the pillows, Simon slowly leaned forward. Claire sank backward, her heart slamming to a halt before jolting back to life.

"Simon."

"How I have ached to taste your lips, my little cat," he murmured. "You make my blood burn."

Angling his dark head, he captured her mouth in a possessive kiss. She shivered, longing to open her lips and deepen the caress. How would it feel to be ravished by this man? To forget what was right or wrong and just allow the surging emotions to wash over her. He moaned deep in his throat, and with a sharp stab of panic at the knowledge of how easy it would be to succumb to his advances, Claire forced her hands to press against his wide chest in protest.

"Simon . . ."

Moving back a fraction, Simon allowed his

gaze to linger on the lips still warm from his touch.

"Yes, Claire?"

"You must halt," she breathed.

He slowly smiled. "Must I?"

"Yes."

"But I quite enjoy kissing you."

And despite all sense, she thoroughly enjoyed being kissed, Claire acknowledged with a flare of unease.

"All the more reason you should not do it."

His chuckle sent a tingle down her spine.

"What absurd logic, my dear."

The dark head began to lower, and Claire felt her resolve melting.

"Simon . . ."

Lost in each other, Simon and Claire never noted the elderly woman sliding sideways in the large chair. It was not until a loud snore ripped through the silence that they abruptly recalled they were not alone.

Waking herself up, Aunt Jane bolted upright.

"What? Who the blazes is making that infernal noise?"

Thirteen

The next morning Claire lay upon the bed and brooded upon her long and restless night. What was the matter with her? she sternly chided. Lord Challmond was not the first handsome gentleman she had ever encountered. He was not even the most charming. So why, then, did she melt like a giddy schoolgirl every time he touched her?

There was no reasonable explanation, she at last conceded.

He was simply one of those gentlemen blessed with the talent to seduce the fairer sex, and much as she might wish to consider herself above such foolishness, she was clearly no less susceptible than any other silly miss.

Not an extraordinarily comforting thought, she acknowledged with a sigh. Before Simon's return to Devonshire she had taken great pride in her cool disregard for childish flirtations. Her mind was concerned with lofty, noble causes that left no interest in common dalliances. It was difficult to accept that she was not nearly so lofty and noble as she believed. Indeed, she was startlingly wanton given the opportunity.

Claire grimaced. At least Simon had belatedly appeared to realize how inappropriately he had been behaving. After the rude interruption by Aunt Jane he had disappeared from her chamber in an oddly stiff fashion. As if he had been as shaken as she was by the fierce flare of passion that had burned between them. Absurd, of course, considering he had no doubt possessed dozens of mistresses. Then he had made only a brief visit after dinner to wish her a pleasant night.

Now she discovered herself awaiting his arrival with a mixed sense of dread and anticipation.

Would he be the charming companion? The intellectual sparring partner? The irresistible seducer? Or the aloof host?

And could she face him without thinking of how it felt to be in his arms?

Chastising her wayward thoughts, Claire was on the point of ringing for the maid and requesting a book from the library, when her solitude was ended by the arrival of a stocky, dark-haired gentleman.

"Mr. Lockmeade." She smiled, relieved to have her brooding thoughts distracted. Besides which, she genuinely liked the uncomplicated gentleman.

"Please, call me Locky," he insisted. "May I join you?"

Despite the fact that Aunt Jane had yet to make her appearance, Claire waved a slender hand toward the chair next to her bed. It never occurred to her that this gentleman was anything but trustworthy. Not only was his character etched in the rugged strength of his countenance, but she possessed an unwavering belief that Simon would never choose a friend who did not possess his same inherent goodness.

"Certainly."

He moved to settle himself in the chair, his gaze lingering on the violent colors still marring her temple.

"How do you feel?"

"Much improved," she assured him.

"You gave me quite a scare," he informed her in stern tones.

She smiled with rueful humor. From all reports, she had set the entire household on its head by her unexpected arrival.

"I fear I have not had the opportunity to thank you. Goodness knows how long I might have lain there if you had not come along."

"I am only relieved that you were not seriously injured."

Her smile widened. "Thank goodness for my thick head, eh?"

He laughed and reached into his pocket to withdraw a folded piece of paper.

"I have brought you a surprise," he announced, handing her the paper.

With distinct curiosity Claire gingerly opened the paper to discover a painting of what might have been herself and several stick forms. Lifting her head, she surveyed Locky with raised brows.

"It is . . . lovely."

"I unfortunately cannot take credit," he swiftly corrected her. "The children at the orphanage asked that I bring it to you."

She felt a prick of surprise. "You were at the orphanage?"

Locky shrugged, but there was a hint of embarrassment in his manner.

"Yes, I have been attempting to lend a bit of help while you recover. Not that I could ever hope to fill your position."

Claire regarded him with growing admiration. How many gentlemen would willingly give their time to an orphanage?

"That is very, very kind of you."

He waved aside her words. "I have discovered that I enjoy spending time with the children."

"I am certain they appreciate having you take such an interest."

He appeared eager to brush aside his good deed, as if he were uneasy at her compliments.

"They miss you."

Not any more than she missed them, she acknowledged with a pang. Their lively chatter and ceaseless questions were just what she needed to divert her inward restlessness.

"And what of Lord Challmond?" She could not prevent the question. "Does he not object to your spending your visit at the orphanage?"

Locky gave a sudden laugh. "Lord Challmond has been far too occupied to concern himself with my whereabouts."

"Oh." It was Claire's turn to struggle with embarrassment. For the first time, she realized that Simon had indeed spent little time with his companion. "I am sorry to have interrupted your stay with Lord Challmond."

"Do not apologize," Locky insisted. "I have never known Simon to be content enough to remain in one place for such a length of time."

Claire frowned in bewilderment. What on earth was he speaking of?

"But Simon lived in London for years."

"According to his friends, it was never in one place," Locky explained. "He would remain at his town house for a week, perhaps two, and then he would be off with Philip and Barth on some lark or another. Almost as if he feared becoming settled." There was a pause as he considered her pale features. "But since coming to Devonshire, he has been almost at peace."

Claire shifted uneasily beneath his regard. Surely he was not implying that she was somehow responsible for Simon remaining in Devonshire? He could not be more off the mark.

"This is his home." She pointed out.

"And what is home?" Locky demanded. "Is it a place or is it a feeling?"

Claire briefly considered his words. Blakewell Manor was certainly her home, but while she possessed a sense of appreciation for the familiar mortar and stones, it was indeed her father and the staff who had helped to raise her that she loved.

"I suppose it is a feeling," she slowly admitted. "And what of you, Locky? Do you have someplace to call home?"

"I hope to someday very soon."

Wondering if he had someone or someplace already in mind, Claire was halted in asking the question as a familiar tingle of awareness had her abruptly turning toward the door.

As expected, Simon was filling the doorway with his large frame. Who else could create that disturbing flutter deep in her heart by merely being near? And as expected, he was elegantly attired in an indigo-blue coat and yellow breeches that set off his well-toned muscles to perfection. What was not expected was the deep scowl that marred his handsome features as he absorbed the obvious comfort between Claire and his best friend.

"Simon," she murmured, her expression wary.

"Good morning, Claire." His glittering gaze turned to Locky. "Am I intruding?"

Locky slowly rose to his feet, his heavy features set in stoic lines.

"Do not be a fool, Challmond," he growled.

The two men regarded each other in prickly silence before Simon gave a sharp shake of his head.

"Forgive me," he muttered. "Mr. Cassel is here to see you, Claire."

Uncertain what had occurred between the gentlemen, Claire breathed an audible sigh. At least she would be freed from this infernal bed. She was far too active to take this enforced bed rest in stride. She longed to be up and about.

"Thank goodness."

She missed Simon's rueful grimace as he stepped aside and the small, rapidly balding surgeon bustled into the room.

"Here we are, then," he proclaimed, bending to inspect Claire's wound without batting an eye at the fact that Claire had obviously been entertaining a gentleman in the bedchamber.

As if realizing the impropriety of his presence, Locky gave a brief bow.

"I shall make myself scarce. Until later, Miss Blakewell."

"Good day, Mr. Lockmeade," she murmured, flinching as the surgeon pressed against her bruise.

"Mmm . . ." Mr. Cassel narrowed his gaze. "Any dizziness?"

Not as long as Simon was not kissing her,

she acknowledged even as she gave a firm shake of her head.

"No."

"No fainting?"

"No."

"No fever?"

"No."

He held her lids wide to peer deeply into her eyes. "You are eating well?"

"Yes."

"Hmmm." At last satisfied, he stepped back, his expression one of disapproval, as if holding her fully responsible for her accident. "It seems that you have been quite fortunate, young lady."

Claire's eyes brightened. "Then I can get up?"

"Yes, but I still wish you to take care for the next few days," he warned. "No more banging your head."

Claire gave a sudden laugh. "Believe me, I shall do my best."

"See that you do."

Suddenly Simon moved farther into the room, his dark features unreadable as he studied Claire's pleased countenance.

"Thank you, Mr. Cassel. Mrs. King will see you out," he murmured, then, waiting for the surgeon to make his bow and hurry from the room, he slowly strolled to tower over the bed. "Well, it appears that you have been released from the jail."

Suddenly realizing that being allowed to rise from her bed also meant she no longer had a reason to remain in Simon's home, Claire battled an absurd, thoroughly unexpected stab of regret.

No, she told herself sternly, she could not wish to remain at Westwood Park. Or to be close to Lord Challmond. It had to be a lingering . . . malaise. A reaction to her severe blow to the head.

What other explanation could there be?

"Yes, indeed." She forced a light tone. "If you will call for a maid, then I can be dressed and on my way."

The emerald eyes narrowed. "In such a hurry, Claire?"

She would rather have her tongue removed than admit she was in no hurry at all.

"There is little point in postponing my leave-taking. I am certain you shall be relieved to be rid of your unwanted guest."

"Do not be so certain. We have, after all, enjoyed the past two days, have we not?"

"Yes, but . . ." Her voice trailed away in bewilderment.

"Perhaps I shall lock you in this bedchamber and toss away the key."

She caught her breath as they gazed at each other for a disturbing moment. Then, with an effort, she lowered her head. He was merely jesting. He would no doubt be delighted to see the back of her.

"You are being foolish," she murmured.

There was a long pause. "Yes, perhaps I am," he at last admitted. "Claire . . ."

With reluctance she lifted her head. "Yes?"

"I . . ." He appeared oddly hesitant, as if uncertain what he wished to say, then, with an abrupt frown, he took a decisive step backward. "It is nothing. I shall fetch your maid."

Not certain what she expected, Claire experienced a queer sense of disappointment as he gave her a small bow and left the chamber.

So that was that. She was free to go, and as she had predicted, Simon was eager to be rid of her.

There was no reason at all to feel as if she should bury her head in the pillow and cry like a wounded child.

Three days later Claire was seated in the empty schoolroom of the orphanage, sorting a box full of books that had been donated by a local merchant. It was a task that unfortunately took little concentration, and for what seemed to be the hundredth time her renegade thoughts turned to Lord Challmond.

He seemed to have simply disappeared.

With every passing hour Claire had expected him to appear. After all, he had haunted her for days, even weeks. He was always popping in when she least expected him. And certainly she assumed that he would wish to assure himself that she was recovering.

But day after day passed without a word, and Claire discovered herself growingly vexed with his lack of attention.

What was the matter with her? she silently chided. She had wished Simon in Jericho when he had pestered her with his persistent presence. Then the moment he had behaved with a bit of decorum, she felt oddly abandoned.

There seemed no means of pleasing her, she reluctantly acknowledged. She could only wish she could return to the contentment that had been hers before Lord Challmond's return to Devonshire.

The sound of the door opening had Claire turning about to discover Harry entering the room and awkwardly crossing the stone floor to join her. With an effort Claire conjured a smile.

"Good morning, Harry."

"Morning, Miss Blakewell." He shifted uneasily before thrusting out his hand. "I have something for you."

Claire reached out to take the smooth rock that Harry offered.

"Why, thank you, Harry. It is lovely."

"It is a magic rock," he confessed in low tones.

"Magic?"

"Aye." He nodded his head in a vigorous

fashion. "It will protect you from the bad blokes."

Clearly the rumors of Mr. Foster had made their way through the neighborhood, and Claire felt a warmth fill her heart at the child's concern.

"I see."

Harry squared his thin shoulders. "I t'ain't need it now that I live here."

She studied the freckled face. "And you are happy here, Harry?"

A wide grin abruptly split the homely face. "I reckon I t'ain't never been so happy."

"I am very pleased."

His grin faintly faded. "And I promise that I won't disappoint you, Miss Blakewell."

Claire was suddenly struck by his solemn words. She recalled Simon's sense of duty and obligation that had haunted his life. She did not wish to see Harry burdened in the same manner.

"You could never disappoint me, Harry." She assured him with a smile. "I only wish you to be happy."

"Harry." Ann entered the room, regarding the pair of them with raised brows. "You are about to miss lunch."

"Blimey." With wiry speed Harry darted out of the room, his footsteps echoing down the hallway.

Gently laughing at Harry's antics, Ann crossed toward Claire.

"I wondered where you had disappeared to. How are you feeling?"

She was not going to admit that she had deliberately been avoiding Ann.

"I feel quite recovered."

The dark gaze deliberately lingered on the pale features and sleepless circles beneath her eyes.

"Then you must feel remarkably better than you appear."

"I am fine," Claire insisted.

"Well, Mr. Foster has a great deal to answer for," Ann retorted, her gaze moving to the fading bruise. "Of course, he has no doubt learned to regret his scandalous behavior. It could not have been comfortable knowing that Lord Challmond's entire staff was searching for him or that the earl had threatened to have him hung from the nearest tree. He is fortunate that he was discovered by the magistrate."

Claire determinedly kept her countenance smooth. It was far too tempting to presume that Simon's outrage was more than neighborly concern at a villain being on the loose in the area.

"I am only relieved that he can no longer be a threat to others."

Ann picked up a leather-bound book, her manner determinedly casual.

"And speaking of Lord Challmond, I believe he should be here any moment."

Claire felt her heart falter. "Here? Why?"

"I mentioned your suggestion of adding a greenhouse to the orphanage, and he wishes to bring Mr. Davis along and discover if it would be a viable plan." Ann slowly lifted her head to study Claire's heated countenance. "I thought you would be pleased?"

Pleased? How could she be pleased when Simon was bound to assume that she had coerced Ann into luring him to the orphanage? It was, after all, what he had learned to expect from women.

And even worse was the fierce, undeniable realization of just how badly she wished to see him. To view his countenance. To hear his voice. To smell that warm, masculine scent.

It sent a shaft of fear straight through her heart.

With a sudden motion she was on her feet. "I fear I cannot."

Ann regarded her in surprise. "No?"

"I . . . am expected home for lunch."

"You could send along a note with your groom," the older woman pointed out in reasonable tones. "This is, after all, what you have wanted to achieve for years."

"Yes, well . . . I really must go," she retorted lamely.

Ann set aside the book and regarded her squarely. "Claire, is there something the matter?"

"No. Nothing at all."

"Are you avoiding Lord Challmond?"

She desperately battled the urge to blush. She did not know what she was doing. And that, of course, was the trouble. She wanted to be with Simon, but she didn't. She wished to continue with the life she had chosen, and yet, she felt a restless dissatisfaction deep within her. She wished to turn back the hands of time but realized it was far, far too late.

"Of course I am not attempting to avoid Lord Challmond," she deliberately lied. "I simply promised Father that I would join him today and I have no wish to disappoint him. I can view the plans on another occasion."

Not surprisingly Ann regarded her with a hint of suspicion.

"If you insist."

"I shall return tomorrow."

Without giving Ann an opportunity to respond, Claire rounded the desk and hurried from the room. Ann knew her far too well not to suspect that something was amiss. All Claire could hope was that she would eventually regain her usual composure.

She moved down the hall and out the door to the front courtyard. Glimpsing her waiting carriage, she began to cross toward it, only to come to a startled halt as she realized the large mare as well as her groom were missing. With a frown she glanced toward the elder servant tugging at an errant weed.

"Rossen, have you seen my groom?"

The servant jerked his thumb in the direction of the pathway.

"He feared that the horse be coming a bit lame. He is walking it to Blakewell Manor and said he would return directly to collect you."

Blast, she inwardly cursed.

"When did he leave?"

"Not more than a moment ago."

Now what did she do?

It would be half an hour or more for the groom to return. Certainly not before Simon would arrive with the builder.

Did she wait here and face him, or ignore all practical sense and walk home?

It took only a moment to decide.

She had walked home hundreds of times without incident. And Mr. Foster had been captured several days before. There was no need to linger here like a helpless child.

Not when to linger meant encountering Lord Challmond.

She would go to great lengths to avoid such an event.

Great lengths, indeed.

With a toss of her head Claire determinedly began marching toward the path through the woods.

Fourteen

Simon ducked beneath the low branch and narrowly missed the large puddle that blocked the path. Gads, why did he not simply call for his carriage to take him to the orphanage? It would certainly have been a great deal faster, not to mention a great deal kinder to his Weston-cut coat and once-glossy Hessians. But then, he had futilely hoped that the walk would clear his muddled thoughts.

A ridiculous hope, of course.

For the past three days he had attempted every method to rid himself of the memory of Miss Blakewell.

He had closeted himself for hours with the new steward to discuss the changes he wished to be made to Westwood Park. He had co-erced Locky into halfhearted games of chess. He had drowned himself in brandy. He had even ridden to the village with the thoughts of seducing the local barmaid, only to return to Westwood Park with the certain knowledge she would never be capable of conjuring his passion.

It was as if he had been . . . bewitched, he seethed as he marched down the narrow path.

From the moment he had held Claire in his arms and leaned her back into the soft pillows, he realized his danger.

Suddenly the game ended and a sharp, savage desire to keep this woman in his home, in his bed had consumed him. It took every bit of his strength not to sweep her off to his chamber and lock the door against the world.

At least he possessed the sense to realize his folly, he tried to reassure himself. With a desperate sense of self-preservation he retreated behind a mask of cool civility. He even allowed Claire to leave Westwood Park without her ever suspecting the cost to himself.

Perhaps absurdly he presumed that her return to Blakewell Manor would ease his discomfort. Instead, he discovered her memory haunting his every thought. Each room he walked in he longed to see her seated upon a chair or standing beside the window. Each night his blood burned with an unfamiliar need.

And if the truth be known, it was only stubborn pride that kept him from camping upon the doorstep of Blakewell Manor.

Fool, fool, fool, he chided, angry with both himself and Claire for putting him in this godawful position.

He should never have come to Devonshire, he told himself. He should have remained in

London and found a beautiful mistress to soothe his restless soul.

Thoroughly vexed, Simon was paying little heed to his surroundings, and it was not until too late that he noted the slender frame rounding the corner at the same moment as himself.

With an instinctive motion he reached out to grasp the tiny woman as they roughly collided. A startled scream echoed through the trees, and Simon pulled back to regard the wide, startled blue eyes with angry disbelief.

Claire Blakewell all alone in the woods . . . again.

By God, did the woman never learn?

"Oh." She breathed in obvious relief. "It is you."

Belatedly realizing his hands were lingering on the warmth of her back, he made a sharp move backward to glare at her in open disapproval.

"What the devil are you doing here?"

Her relief abruptly faded at his sharp tone, and a decidedly icy expression settled on her countenance.

"Attempting to walk home."

"By yourself?"

Her chin tilted. "Obviously."

"Good God," he breathed in exasperation. He had promised himself that he would treat this woman with a cool disregard. That he would train himself to view her as a mere neighbor. But there was no preventing his violent reaction to her bloody-minded stupidity.

She had already been attacked once. Would she not be satisfied until she had been ravished or even killed? The thought was enough to twist his heart in horror.

"Do you not possess any sense at all?"

Typically her reaction was one of denial at her childish behavior.

"I beg your pardon?"

"You heard me," he growled. "Less than a week ago you were attacked and nearly killed. I thought even someone as ill tempered and unreasonable as you would have learned your lesson."

"In case you have forgotten, Mr. Foster is in the hands of the magistrate."

How could he forget? He had paid a small fortune to ensure the blackguard had gone from the magistrate straight to a boat headed for the West Indies.

"And you presume that he is the only villain in all of England?"

"These woods are hardly crawling with desperate criminals," she retorted.

His expression hardened. "It takes only one."

Something flashed deep in her eyes before her chin was tilting even higher.

"Fine. You have made your point, my lord. Now, you must excuse me."

She expected him to step aside and meekly allow her to continue on her way?

"Why are you so bloody stubborn?"

"Me?" Her mouth dropped in disbelief. "I am not the one constantly meddling in others' lives."

"Only those too bacon-brained to keep themselves out of danger."

"I do not need your help, Lord Challmond."

"I will not allow you to wander through the countryside alone."

"Allow me?" Her voice rose in outrage. "May I remind you, sir, that you have no right to decide whether or not I wander the countryside alone?"

The realization that she was absolutely right did nothing to ease his temper. What did he care of rights? She was fortunate he did not toss her over his shoulder and carry her off to be locked in his wine cellar.

"Someone needs to take charge of you," he retorted. "You are like an unruly child with no nanny to keep you from tumbling into disaster."

She was nearly trembling with fury. "I am a grown woman who has been taking care of myself for a good many years."

He snorted his lack of approval. "More luck than skill, I wager."

"That is enough." She slapped her hands onto her hips. "I will not have you treat me as if I am some half-witted child."

"Then stop behaving as one."

Their gazes clashed in open battle.

"Stand aside, Lord Challmond."

His eyes narrowed. "I am escorting you back to Blakewell Manor."

"No, you are not," she denied in fierce tones. "I may have endured your companionship in an absurd attempt to fool my father, but that does not give you the right to order me about. Indeed, from this moment on I have no desire to see you again."

Simon was struck by a savage stab of pain he had not experienced since the day they had taken him from his mother's arms.

Shocked and disturbed by his reaction, Simon discovered himself striking out like a wounded child.

"Why, you ungrateful vixen."

Her lips quivered before she thinned them to determined lines.

"Ungrateful because I am not groveling with delight at the notion of being bullied by the notorious Lord Challmond?"

All at once Simon had endured enough. This woman had tangled him into knots since his arrival in Devonshire. She had used him for her devious games, stirred his passions with her kisses, and driven him nearly to Bedlam with her thorough lack of regard for her own safety. And worse of all, she had managed to creep into his every thought.

No woman had ever disrupted his life in such a fashion.

"Very well. You wish to place yourself at the

mercy of every cutpurse in the area, then so be it. Do not expect sympathy from me when your throat is slit."

"I have never asked for your sympathy. Indeed, all I wish from you is that you would return to London, where you clearly belong."

Simon stilled at the brittle words.

"You wish me to leave Westwood Park?"

There was a pause as the blue eyes appeared to darken with what might have been pain. But even as the thought crossed his mind, her expression tightened.

"Yes. That is precisely what I wish."

"Very well. Let it never be said that I did not do whatever necessary to please a lady," he gritted out with a mocking bow. "I will leave on the morrow. Good day."

With his head held high he stepped around her frozen frame and continued on the path to the orphanage.

Why should he not return to London? There was nothing to keep him here. And God alone knew that he would travel to India if it would take him away from Miss Blakewell.

He would go to London, and Claire Blakewell be damned.

As expected, the streets of London were uncomfortably crowded. Deftly avoiding a lumbering carriage and the several dirty urchins who darted dangerously between the horses,

Simon pulled to a halt in front of Boodles. He signaled to his groom, and leaping onto the pavement, he left the Tilbury in his servant's capable hands.

It had been less than two weeks since his return to London, and already he wearied of the noise, the smells, and endless visitors who filled his elegant town house.

Over and over his thoughts turned back to Devonshire. Was his steward repairing Mrs. Foley's cottage? Was Harry minding his studies? Was Locky, who had remained behind, assisting Mr. Davis as he prepared to start the greenhouse?

And, of course, the inevitable thoughts of Claire Blakewell.

Blast the woman.

He had never before worried over the plight of his estate. He paid others to deal with such troubles. His only concern should be whether Weston had finished his coat or if he should choose the opera dancer or the exquisite widow to warm his bed that evening.

Instead, he had ignored his numerous invitations to the vast array of entertainments and the more personal invitation from his one-time mistress and chosen the gentlemen's club. He wished only for a good brandy, a quiet corner, and time to brood on his ill fortunes.

Stepping forward, he allowed the silver-haired servant to pull open the door.

"My lord, what a delightful surprise."

"Thank you, Huber. I wish a comfortable seat, a large quantity of brandy, and no distractions."

"Of course."

There was something in the servant's expression that made Simon's brow rise.

"Yes, Huber?"

Huber cleared his throat. "I thought you would wish to know that Lord Brasleigh has been gracious enough to join us this evening."

"Damn." Despite his close bonds to Philip, Simon was in no mood for companionship. Still, he could hardly insult him by ignoring his presence. "I suppose I should make my bow."

"As you say, my lord."

Simon heaved a sigh. "Lead the way."

"Very good."

With a nod of his head Huber entered the club and led Simon toward the distant corner of the large room, where a tall, dark-haired gentleman with silver eyes sat staring into the fireplace with a decidedly grim expression. Simon was startled to discover his friend appeared as weary and ill used as he felt.

At his approach, Philip abruptly lifted his head to regard him with a fierce scowl. The scowl was only mildly tempered by the realization of who was intruding upon his privacy.

"Good God, Simon," he said. "What the devil are you doing here? I thought you were in the wilds of Devonshire?"

"I was," Simon retorted with a grimace. "And I must warn you that my travels have left me in a foul mood."

"It cannot be any more foul than my own." He waved a slender hand toward the wing chair on the opposite side of the fireplace. "Have a seat."

Giving up hope for the solitude he had craved, Simon settled his tall frame into the supple leather and motioned for the hovering servant.

"Your best brandy," he commanded. "And plenty of it."

"Yes, my lord." The uniformed man bowed and walked toward a heavy side table. In a blink of an eye he returned with a crystal-cut decanter and glass.

"Devonshire not all that you wished?" Philip demanded as Simon poured himself a healthy measure of the amber liquid and tossed it down his throat.

"Devonshire was fine. It was my ill-tempered, shrew of a neighbor that was impossible."

Philip's elegantly handsome features tightened. "A female, I presume?"

Simon poured another measure of brandy. "Claire, the bloody cat."

Philip gave a startled blink. "Pardon me?"

"Miss Blakewell," Simon explained, the image of a pale countenance and impossibly blue eyes making his heart ache in the strangest manner. "An unruly, ungrateful spitfire with the manners of a street urchin."

"Did I not warn you that it was safer to battle Napoleon than to battle the wiles of a cunning female?"

"I will certainly drink to that." Simon polished off his glass, hoping to drown the memory of Claire Blakewell. Why the devil could she not leave him in peace? "What of you? How could your mood be foul, when you have been surrounded by the comforts of London and the lovely charm of Miss Ravel?"

"Unfortunately I just returned to London. I was called away."

"Called away to where?"

"Surrey."

Simon didn't bother to hide his surprise. "Good God, why?"

Philip's expression grew bleak. "My ward."

"Ah." Simon recalled Philip's occasional reference to Miss Lowe. "I thought she resided in Bath?"

There was a sharp, humorless laugh. "It is a long, unfortunate tale. Let it just be said that at the moment I would like nothing better than to lock her in a cellar and toss away the key."

"Here. Here." Simon poured another glass of brandy and lifted it in a mocking toast. "To deep cellars with thick doors and—"

A sudden disruption across the room brought Simon's words to a halt, and he

turned to discover Huber discreetly attempting
to turn away a large, decidedly bosky lord. Simon rose to his feet at the same moment as
Philip as they both recognized the chestnut
hair and hazel eyes of Lord Wickton.

"Stand aside, Huber," Lord Wickton commanded in loud tones.

The servant held up his hands in a pleading
motion. "My lord, please."

Barth swayed unsteadily. "Stand aside or be
prepared to defend yourself."

"Good God," Philip muttered as he hurried
across the floor to place an arm around his
friend's shoulders. "Wickton, come along."

Barth Juston, Earl of Wickton, allowed himself to be led across the room, not even pro-
testing as Simon pressed him into the wing
chair.

"Challmond? Brasleigh?" He blinked in
muddled surprise. "What the devil are you doing here?"

"Clearly the same thing you have been doing for quite some time," Simon retorted in
dry tones.

Barth turned toward him, his fuzzy gaze
landing on the decanter beside the chair.

"Ah . . . brandy. Just what I need."

"Coffee," Philip said as he whisked the spir-
its out of the reach of the foxed nobleman
and handed it to the hovering Huber. "Now,
why are you not in Kent with your new bride?"

An unnaturally bitter expression twisted Barth's countenance.

"There is no bride."

Simon regarded his friend in surprise. "I thought the marriage was arranged?"

"As did I." Barth's head flopped onto the soft leather, his lids fluttering shut in weary pain. "Unfortunately the bride has decided that she prefers another. And I must say, I do not blame her. He is an absolutely brilliant gentleman without a fault to be discovered. And believe me, I have tried."

Simon and Philip shared a knowing glance, both recalling Barth's fervent distaste in being forced up the aisle by necessity.

"That is rather a bad break, but she is not the only maiden in England. You will soon find another bride," Philip drawled.

Barth slowly raised his gaze and Simon felt a stab of unease. There was something barren and desolate in those hazel eyes. As if he had lost something priceless. Was that the same barren pain that haunted him in the late hours of the night?

"Oh, yes, there are no doubt any number of maidens willing to become the Countess of Wickton." He grimaced. "A pity I do not bloody well want them."

Philip gave another humorless laugh. "Well, are we not a sad trio? What happened to the Casanova Club? Love them, and leave them wishing for more?"

"It is all that Gypsy's fault," Barth muttered. "Her and her devil's curse."

"Absurd." Simon gave a shake of his head.

Barth stabbed him with a jaundiced glare. "Then, you have not tumbled into the stormy seas of love?"

"Love?" Simon grimaced even as his stomach clenched with a sickening sense of dread.

No.

He couldn't be in love.

For God's sake, he didn't even believe in the ludicrous emotion. And if he did, surely love was a gentle, warm emotion that brought pleasure to a person, not this burning ache that gnawed at his guts?

Still, what other explanation could there be?

He could not sleep, he had no interest in his usual pursuits, in his friends, or even his mistress. His thoughts refused to turn from Miss Blakewell. And even when he was miles away he had only to close his eyes to recall the scent of her skin and the feel of her satin mouth.

Most telling of all was the knowledge that he had not left Devonshire because he wished to be in London, but because he could no longer be at Westwood Park without Claire at his side.

Lord, what a fool he had been. A blind, bloody fool.

He had been running for years to postpone the duty that awaited him like a noose of inevitability. He had never considered the possibility that duty could be so amazingly delightful. That he could care so deeply for his tenants and neighbors. That he could love the woman who would become Countess of Challmond.

That he could at last find . . . home.

"My lord."

With a startled blink Simon turned to discover a servant hovering at his side with an anxious expression.

"Yes?"

"A message has been delivered for you."

"Thank you." Simon accepted the sealed note and broke it open with a faint frown.

Simon,

> *Thought you should know that Miss Stewart will be leaving for Wiltshire within the month. Miss Blakewell will no doubt join her unless someone halts her from leaving Devonshire.*

> *Locky*

Scanning the neatly scrawled message, Simon abruptly crumpled it into a ball and tossed it into the fire.

"Damnation."

"Troubles?" Philip demanded in concern.

"It is from Locky."

"Locky?" Barth hiccuped. "Where the devil is he?"

"Devonshire." Simon clenched his fists. "I have to leave."

"Wait." Philip placed a hand on his shoulder, his expression somber. "Is there something we can do to help?"

Simon met the silver gaze with a determined smile. "As a matter of fact, you can wish me luck," he said, as he came to a sudden decision. "I am off to win the heart of the woman I love."

Fifteen

It was one of those rare, perfect spring days. A flood of sunlight warmed the wide terrace, spreading through the tidy garden and dancing off the fountains. Overhead the sky was a vast canvas of blue, unspoiled by even a hint of clouds.

Unfortunately, Claire possessed little appreciation for the fine weather. Instead, she paced across the terrace with a restless sense of dissatisfaction.

Blast, Lord Challmond. Blast, blast, blast.

His return to London was supposed to have ended her torment. With him gone, her life could return to normal, and he would be no more than a distant memory.

But instead of the peace she had expected, she had discovered herself plagued with regrets.

Why had she told him that she wished him to leave Devonshire? That she wished never to see him again?

Because she had been afraid, she acknowledged with a flare of disgust. She had been utterly henhearted and unable to face the truth.

Even now she found herself unable to thoroughly accept the vast jumble of emotions that battled within her. How did one comprehend the terrible sense of loss? The feeling that a part of one's heart was dying? And yet harbor a queer tingle of delight at having been kissed by the only man she would ever love.

Yes, love, she had reluctantly conceded. That giddy, foolish emotion she had intended to avoid at all cost. How it had happened she did not know; she was not sure she even cared. She was only certain that as the days had slowly passed, she had been forced to search her heart and discover the truth.

She loved Simon Townsled, seventh Earl of Challmond.

She loved his swift sense of the ridiculous, his intelligence, his kind heart and inner strength. She loved how he smiled deep into her eyes, as if they shared a secret only they understood. And she loved how he made her shiver with the heat of his desire.

But in her fear she had struck out to push him away. She did not want to be in love. And certainly not with a gentleman who considered her an ill-tempered, unmanageable shrew.

Not until too late did she discover that no amount of distance, no amount of denial, and no amount of wishing things had been different could change her emotions. She might not want to be in love. She might long to pattern her life after Ann Stewart, but there was no avoiding the truth. It did not even matter that Simon in no way returned her feelings.

It was all a horrible, horrible muddle.

Hearing the sound of approaching footsteps, Claire hurriedly composed her features. She was well aware that her subdued manner and drawn countenance had been noted by those around. She only hoped to divert the questions she could detect glinting in their eyes.

Slowly turning, Claire watched as Ann stepped through the open French windows and swept toward her with a warm smile.

"Claire . . . there you are."

"Ann."

Not surprisingly the dark gaze lingered on the shadows beneath Claire's eyes and the noticeable droop of her soft mouth.

"Are you not feeling well?"

"I am fine."

Ann lifted her brows in disbelief. "You look terrible."

"Thank you," Claire retorted in dry tones.

"Are you certain that you do not wish for me to call for a surgeon?"

"I am fine," Claire insisted with a sigh. Unless the surgeon possessed the means of removing her heart, there was no cure for her ills. "Is there something you need?"

Ann paused as if considering whether to insist on procuring Mr. Cassel, then, with a small shrug, she allowed herself to be diverted.

"Actually I came bearing good news."

"Oh?"

An undeniable glow entered Ann's lovely face. "I have received a letter from Lady Welbrock."

Claire gave a faint frown as she attempted to place the name. "I do not believe I am acquainted with her."

"She is a prominent contributor to several charities and has lately collected a group of ladies who are interested in our efforts here," Ann readily explained.

Claire realized that she was being slow-witted, but she was finding it inordinately difficult to follow her friend's evident excitement.

"I do not understand."

"They would like to open an orphanage similar to ours in Wiltshire. They are willing to contribute the money if we will help them get it established."

"You mean go to Wiltshire?" Claire retorted in disbelief.

"Of course."

"Oh."

Ann closely surveyed her expression of startled unease.

"It is what we have discussed for some time," she pointed out in gentle tones.

It was true. For years they had discussed the possibility of traveling throughout England to help the unfortunate children. It was what she had always dreamed of. But now that the time was here, Claire discovered herself withdrawing from the mere thought of leaving Devonshire.

To go to Wiltshire meant that she might never see Simon again. How could she possibly bear it? At least if she remained here she could console herself with the thought that Simon might visit Westwood Park. A glimpse of him was surely better than nothing at all?

A grim smile twisted her lips. Was there not the old saying, How the mighty are fallen? She was in a sorry state indeed.

Realizing that Ann was awaiting her response, she forced a faint smile to her mouth.

"Yes, I suppose."

A mysterious glint entered the dark eyes. "You do not seem as pleased as I thought you would be."

"It is just such a surprise."

Ann inspected her guarded expression. "You do wish to go, do you not?"

"I . . ." Unable to lie beneath that knowing gaze, Claire abruptly turned away and crossed to the low stone railing. "What of Father?"

"I presumed his marriage to Mrs. Mayer was all but announced," Ann retorted in surprise. "What better reason to wish to be in Wiltshire?"

Claire shuddered, but not even the thought of Lizzy could drive her from Devonshire.

"I shall have to give it consideration, Ann." She cowardly avoided giving a direct answer.

"Of course." There was a pause. "Why do I not return later in the week?"

"Yes. Thank you."

Claire listened as Ann slowly crossed the terrace and returned to the house. She had no doubt the older woman was puzzled by her lack of enthusiasm. After all, if she had made the same pronouncement two months earlier, Claire would have been overjoyed. Certainly she would never have hesitated at agreeing to travel to Wiltshire.

But how could she explain?

The plain truth was she couldn't. Not without confessing the truth of her feelings, something she had no intention of doing, with Ann or anyone else.

It was only moments later when the sound of the footsteps once again echoed through the air. With a frown Claire reluctantly turned back toward the French doors.

Had Ann forgotten something? Or was it yet another servant attempting to coerce her into eating?

She stiffened in horror. It was not Ann, nor even a servant, who was standing in the doorway and regarding her with an unreadable expression. Her heart gave a violent lurch as her gaze swept over the dark features that haunted her dreams and the decidedly masculine frame encased in a coat of Clarence blue and cream pantaloons.

"You," she breathed, uncertain if he was indeed there or a vision of her battered heart. "What are you doing here?"

Proving he was very much real, Simon moved forward, not halting until he was standing close enough for her to feel the heat from his body.

"I have come for you," he announced in firm tones.

She gave a startled blink. "What?"

"Please, can we sit?"

Decidedly dazed, she gave a vague nod. "If you wish."

Taking her arm, Simon led her to the marble bench, then, ensuring she was comfortably settled, he lowered himself beside her. His hand slid down her arm to grasp her nerveless fingers. She quivered, all too conscious of the warmth of his touch and the scent of his male skin.

"Before I explain why I am here, I wish to confess a secret."

She frowned in confusion. "Very well."

"You recall that I told you I was in Italy during the war?" he abruptly demanded.

"Yes."

"While I was there, Philip, Barth, and I stumbled across an old Gypsy woman," he continued, his gaze lowered to where their fingers were interlaced. "She was being beaten by a gang of farmers."

"How awful."

"The three of us frightened away the farmers and led the old woman back to the other Gypsies. Once there, she gave each of us a . . . blessing."

Claire regarded him in bewilderment. She had no notion of why he had returned to Devonshire or why he was revealing his story. She knew only that she wished they could remain like this forever.

"What kind of blessing?"

Something that might have been embarrassment rippled over his handsome countenance.

"That each of us would discover our true love before the heat of summer burned again."

"A typical Gypsy blessing."

"Naturally we laughed aside such nonsense," he agreed. "What did three gentleman such as ourselves care for love?"

"Why do you tell me this?" she asked in soft tones.

His gaze slowly lifted, and she gave a small gasp at the pain smoldering in the emerald depths.

"Because since coming to Devonshire, true love no longer seems like such nonsense."

"Simon . . ."

"Please, let me speak, Claire," he begged in husky tones. "I do not know why I came to

Devonshire. I know only that I have felt restless and in search of peace for years. There was no one I could call family and nowhere to call home. In desperation I simply tried to stay ahead of the emotions that plagued me. Then I encountered a sharp-tongued vixen who made me forget my troubled soul."

She caught her breath, unable to accept what he was saying.

"You treat me as a child."

"I assure you, I never regarded you as a child." His lips twisted with wry humor. "Indeed, there was more than one night I lay awake wishing that I could. Your kisses stirred a desire that was not easily dismissed."

She gazed at him with an unconscious plea in her countenance.

"What do you want from me?"

His hand tightened on her fingers.

"At first I was merely intrigued by your odd behavior. One moment you were thrusting me away and the next you were playing the flirt."

"I explained why," she said with a blush.

"Yes, but while you were honest with me, I was not honest with myself." He paused, his gaze probing deep into her wide eyes. "I told myself that I only wished to discover the reason for your unpredictable manner and perhaps punish you a bit for daring to trifle with the Earl of Challmond. But it was merely an excuse to be with you."

"Why?"

"Because I was falling in love with you."

She stiffened at his blunt confession, wondering if she was losing her wits. She could not possibly have heard him correctly.

"But . . ."

His features abruptly softened at her bemused expression. "What, my darling?"

"You cannot love me."

His brows lifted. "No?"

She gave a slow shake of her head. "As you said, I am an ill-tempered, ill-mannered shrew, and I possess none of the talents a gentleman seeks in a lady."

The emerald eyes flashed with a fierce emotion. "You possess the talents that this gentleman prefers," he assured her. "You are kind, loyal, and generous to those in need."

Those in need . . . Claire gave a sudden gasp.

"Oh."

"What is it?"

"Ann has been offered an opportunity to open an orphanage in Wiltshire," Claire exclaimed. "She wishes me to go with her."

He stilled, regarding her with a searching gaze. "Is it what you wish?"

"I do not know," she answered with an uncharacteristic hint of uncertainty. "All my life I have thought it was my duty to care for others. More than that, I enjoyed knowing that I could make the lives of those around me better."

He lifted her hand to place her fingers against his lean cheek.

"You can make a difference as my wife," he shook her by insisting. "Already you have made me open my heart to my staff and tenants. They are no longer just people who depend upon me for their livelihood, but Mrs. Foley and her damp cottage and Harry with his fear of the blacksmith and Cook who cried when I remembered to give her a small token on her birthday. With you at my side we can accomplish anything you desire."

Wife.

Could it be true?

Could he indeed love her with the same burning intensity that she loved him?

Her heart clenched with poignant excitement, but at the same moment she did not forget the loyalty she owed her best friend.

"But what of Ann?" she demanded. "She will be on her own."

He gave a sudden laugh. "Somehow I doubt that."

"What do you mean?"

"I have the distinct impression that Locky intends to follow Miss Stewart wherever she chooses to go."

Claire felt a flare of disbelief at his words. "Mr. Lockmeade?"

"Yes." He gave a shrug, the emerald eyes dancing with wicked amusement. "If we had not been so distracted with each other, I believe we would have realized there was something going on between them."

Claire recalled Locky's insistence that he enjoyed spending his days at the orphanage, his ready willingness to take the children fishing, his gentle smile as he watched Ann across the room.

"Mr. Lockmeade and Ann?" she murmured.

"Do you disapprove?"

She considered the question before giving a firm shake of her head.

"Not at all. I am just shocked."

"He will be very good to her," Simon promised in low tones.

"Yes, I believe he would."

"But not as good as I will be to you if you will only say you love me." He moved her hand to his lips and gently nuzzled her fingers. "You do love me, do you not?"

She shivered, not quite certain she was thoroughly at ease with the passion he could spark with a simple touch.

"I did not wish to."

"But you do."

His tone was firm, but there was a hint of uncertainty in the proud features that melted her heart.

She might not have planned to love this man, but destiny had chosen her path the moment Simon had returned to Devonshire. She belonged with him. She belonged with him, and there wasn't a blessed thing she could do to change that fact.

"Yes."

"Claire."

An agonized groan rumbled deep in his throat as he lowered his head. With exquisite care he touched his lips to her own, softly urging her mouth to part. Claire shivered as she pressed herself to the wide chest, opening her lips with a gasp of fierce pleasure.

Night after night she had dreamed of being held in his arms, feeling the heat of his searing kisses. But nothing could compare to this moment.

Sensing her surrender, Simon cupped her face with strong hands, deepening his kiss with a moan of satisfaction.

They were lost in a world of pleasure, and it was not until there was a loud cough that they reluctantly pulled away.

Turning her head, Claire discovered her father standing in the center of the terrace with his hands on his hips.

"Here. Here," he scolded. "What is the meaning of this?"

Slowly rising to his feet, Simon regarded the older gentleman with a determined expression.

"I am attempting to convince your daughter to wed me," he announced in blunt tones.

Surprisingly Henry Blakewell merely raised his brows in a mild manner.

"You do not say? Having any luck?"

Simon turned to glance down at the bemused Claire. "Well?"

She forced herself to give a faint shrug. "I suppose I shall have no peace until I do."

Simon gave a shout of laughter. "You are learning, my vixen."

Her father heaved an audible sigh. "Well, at last."

She favored him with a frown. "What?"

"Good God, I thought I would be forced to marry that ghastly woman before you came up to scratch," he complained.

"Marry?" Claire gave a slow shake of her head.

"Yes, marry."

"You mean Lizzy?"

He glared at her in reproach for her slow wits. "Of course I mean Lizzy. Do you honestly believe I would wish to wed a lady with no interest beyond my pocketbook?"

"Then . . . why?"

"All I wished was to frighten you enough to find a husband."

Claire regarded her father in stunned surprise. He did not wish to marry Lizzy? It had all been no more than a cunning device to lure her into marriage?

"Why, you devious old fox," she accused her father in disbelief.

A slow, decidedly sly smile crossed the thin face. "At last I shall have my grandchildren."

A rush of heat stained her cheeks, but it was Simon who responded as he returned to the bench and wrapped an intimate arm about her shoulders.

"I hope not too swiftly," he murmured as he gazed down at her upturned face. "I already share my beloved with tenants, orphans, cats, and any other poor soul who might be in need of help. I would like at least a portion of her time."

"Yes, well . . ." Henry cleared his throat, sensing his presence was unwelcome. "I must call upon Mrs. Mayer. She will wish to resume her flirtation with Mr. Mallot. He does, after all, possess quite a prosperous brewery, if no title. Oh, and do not forget to set a date for the wedding."

Once again lost in each other, Claire and Simon paid little heed as the older gentleman crossed the terrace and disappeared into the house.

Slowly smiling, Simon lifted his hand to stroke the satin softness of her cheek.

> *A love that is true*
> *A heart that is steady*
> *A wounded soul healed*
> *A spirit made ready.*
> *Three women will come*
> *As the seasons will turn*
> *And bring true love to each*
> *Before the summer again burns . . .*

Claire gave a bewildered smile. "What is that?"

"A Gypsy's blessing," he answered as his fingers moved to her soft lips. "Now, about that wedding day, Miss Blakewell."

"The sooner the better, Lord Challmond." Claire raised her hands behind his neck.

"Sooner," he murmured as he angled his head downward. "Definitely sooner."

About the Author

Debbie Raleigh lives with her family in Missouri. Her next Regency romance, *A Bride for Lord Wickton*, which will continue her A Rose for Three Rakes trilogy, will be published in March 2001. Debbie loves to hear from readers, and you may write to her c/o Zebra Books. Please include a self-addressed stamped envelope if you wish a response.

More Zebra Regency Romances

Put a Little Romance in Your Life With
Hannah Howell

Merlin's Legacy

A Series From
Quinn Taylor Evans

<u>BOOK YOUR PLACE ON OUR WEBSITE</u>
<u>AND MAKE THE</u>
<u>READING CONNECTION!</u>

We've created a customized website just for our very special readers, where you can get the inside scoop on everything that's going on with Zebra, Pinnacle and Kensington books.

When you come online, you'll have the exciting opportunity to:

- View covers of upcoming books
- Read sample chapters
- Learn about our future publishing schedule (listed by publication month *and author*)
- Find out when your favorite authors will be visiting a city near you
- Search for and order backlist books from our online catalog
- Check out author bios and background information
- Send e-mail to your favorite authors
- Meet the Kensington staff online
- Join us in weekly chats with authors, readers and other guests
- Get writing guidelines
- AND MUCH MORE!

Visit our website at
http://www.zebrabooks.com